Annie in Hiding

Dedicated to elementary school teachers and Marv Lansing. In the words of retired Superintendent of Eau Claire Public Schools, Dr. Marvin Lansing: "The greatest thing ever for helping troubled young kids is the elementary school teacher.

Author's note.

I have been placing the author's biography at the end of the book. I decided that the reader perhaps would want some insight into the background of who was doing the writing. In the bio, I mention my lack of early education. I think that lack started toward the end of grade four with a very short lesson in long division.

At ten years old, upon returning to school;, I had been playing in the woods for a week or two; the tadpoles were hatching, the snakes and turtles were out, etc. When I went back to school, the teacher handed out a sheet of long division problems. Since I had never seen a long division problem, I turned around and got a quick lesson from a friend, Dee Dailey. (Dee went on to be a teacher.)

In about five minutes, the math lesson was nearly complete, the teacher belted me across the back with a reinforced yardstick. The shock of that blow in that quiet classroom where everyone was watching the teacher descend on me was indescribable. Instantly I wet my pants. When she was back at her desk, I crawled out the door and never went back.

It is a curious thing: I vividly recall learning how to do long division in that brief lesson from Dee, and I have no recollection of a lesson coming from that teacher.

And then, the trouble began. As you will read in the bio, my education from that time through grade eight was nearly nonexistent. After reading the author bio, you, the reader, will also have a little insight into the source of the stories I write.

Wishing Western, A brief biography of Charles Kwick

The pen name J.B. Patel is made up of the scrambled first initials of my seven grandchildren. In this printing I decided to use my name. When I did the scrambling, I had no idea the name Patel was a very common name in India. Your confusion on why one with a name common in India, is writing Westerns is justified.

I am sometimes referred to as a Jack Pine Savage. I guess I come by the nickname honestly since I was born in 1940 in an abandoned logger's cabin replete with a dirt floor near Pearson, Wisconsin. Except for "Two World's Ridge," an Amish love story, and a few other science fiction stories, most of what I write is Western romance. I guess I need those happy endings.

It seems from the time I was born I wished; Western. As a child, I wished for a pair of six guns strapped to my hips, cowboy boots, a cowboy hat, and, of course, horses. I'm in my eighties now; at this time of my life, I've moved to town and left the horses behind, but I still have the boots and the hat. As a city dweller now, I'm still scribbling stories born mostly out of a misspent youth and the painful removal from family at eleven years old.

Where do the stories come from? There were ten in the family; Dad died on the operating table just before his tenth child was born. I was ten when Dad died. I got into skipping school and real estate and exploring; the trouble was, I explored other people's real estate. My brother and I broke into a couple of cabins and made a mess.

Roused from bed the night before, the very next day, on my eleventh birthday, I woke up in a jail cell. That morning, I stood before a judge. In 1951, the judge didn't have to wait for any input from a defense lawyer, social services, psychologists... there were none. By four in the afternoon, eighteen hours after I was caught, I was dropped off at the Wisconsin Child Center in Sparta, Wisconsin. All alone, 'a ward of the state until I turned twenty-one.' Happy eleventh birthday!

The compliments on my writing have centered on my sincerity, passion, and maybe even a little anger, never on my grammar. From grade four to grade eight, I received no education to speak of. So, when it comes to grammar, if you are critical, you will have a good time reading my stories.

Because of its proximity to the railroad, the center was built as a dropping-off spot for orphans in the late 1800s. From the Center's inception to 1933, every Tuesday excess orphans were placed on the orphan train and shipped out West to be adopted or indentured. Thankfully, my time at Sparta missed the Orphan Train era. The center was enlarged and became the temporary home for children of troubled families. I could have been the poster child for troubled children.

At the center, the nights were the hardest. For nearly six years I put myself to sleep with my head on the windowsill daydreaming. My experiences at the Center, my daydreaming, and my imagination are the subjects of many of my stories. Like my childhood experiences, many of my stories include orphans, runaways, the abandoned, or the disenfranchised.

After my stay at the Child Center, I won the lottery. I was able to spend two years at a foster home with a great family, and I met a great gal who I married; she even had horses.

Here in the autumn, or maybe it is the winter of my life, ideas for stories still pop into my head, and I still enjoy scribbling them down. I characterize most of my writing as Western romantic fiction. I've been trying for some time to figure out why my stories must finish with happy endings. As I think back, during the daydreaming while I was cooped up at the Wisconsin Child Center, I had to have happy endings.

One of my favored supervisors at the Wisconsin Child Center, some fifty years later, asked me, "I've often wondered; how did you survive?" I'm guessing those happy endings to my daydreaming helped.

Annie in Hiding

Introduction

Many years ago, I learned that my old home of nearly 6 years, the Wisconsin Child Center at Sparta, Wisconsin, was intentionally built close to the railroad station. The site was chosen so that 'excess' children, numbers greater than the Center was built for, could be put on the Orphan Train. Since then, I have learned of many orphan train stories.

(Excess children were numbers that would allow the diseases in center to spread rapidly.)

For this story I originally considered twins given away at birth, one adopted into a well-to-do family, the other adopted and then orphaned again, sent to an orphanage, then enduring a terrible life. My story would have them somehow meeting at some future time.

In research I reread "The Prince and The Pauper," it was far from what I was considering which was, the coming together of the long-lost twins, not the changing places. Based on my knowledge of such children, I cannot conceive of the twins coming together and trading places and walking away from one another, once they found each other I figured there would be no way they would lose sight of one another.

As a vehicle to bring the twins together I wanted a female, not a relative or one emotionally attached to either, in this case she had to be both mobile, and very noble.

When looking for a background story for my heroine, Annie, I stumbled onto my title while looking at the lyrics to the old song, 'Annie Laurie.' (Sometimes mistaken as a Stephen Foster song.) From there, while looking at Stephen Foster's song, 'Nelly Bly,' I discovered the investigative reporter Nellie Bly. She hid her real identity using the name from the Stephen Foster song with a slightly different spelling.

There are so many terrible circumstances that Orphan Train children were placed in that the meeting of the orphan and 'Annie in Hiding' became simplified, one could pick and choose the circumstance.

I placed them in the Orphan Train era. The train I wanted for story flexibility was completed from coast to coast in 1869 which gave me plenty of flexibility.

The pistol that Annie needed for personal protection for one in her line of work was a Remington Rider. It was built in 1871, a five shot .32 caliber affair which would be very devastating at close range. Given Annie's chosen task and the potential for conflict, she needed protection up close.

The short story; Hangdog Page 121

Since this book is dedicated to Dr. Marvin Lansing, I included the short story Hangdog. The background of the title origin came from one of Marv's expressions and is explained on page 121.

Annie in Hiding

By
Charles Kwick

Annie in Hiding

Part I

Kangaroo court.

Monday, June 2, 1879 Kearney, Nebraska in the courtroom of Judge Odell Swinton.

The bailiff brought a young man into the courtroom in handcuffs; his clothing was tattered, and his shirt pocket was ripped and hanging by a few threads. Still, there seemed to be an aloof quiet strength or dignity that he maintained.

The judge grinned with obvious satisfaction seeing the boy in cuffs; he was anxious to tear into him. To the judge, the fact the lad's clothing was worn, and his shirt pocket was hanging precariously by a few threads gave him satisfaction; secretly he wanted to inflict more damage.

Almost with glee, the judge read from the booking sheet, "You spent the weekend in jail for bludgeoning another. One that just happened to be my son, and breaking his nose…"

"What do you have to say for yourself!?"

The boy in handcuffs figured he was going to come in last place in this battle no matter what he said, so he thought he would make it brief. First, he knew that it was the judge that had put him in jail for the weekend. Which meant if this was likened to a foot race, the judge was already at the finish line, and in his case the decision probably was already made.

In handcuffs he shrugged and stated, “He kept at me; he wouldn’t let me be, he took a hold of me and purposely ripped my shirt… So… I popped him in the nose. It wasn’t much of a fight.”

Incensed at what the Judge figured was flippancy on the part of the boy, the judge snapped, “What’s your name, and where did you come from?”

With a bit of an inward smile, the boy replied, “My name is Tanner free man. I come from back east.”

Again, the judge snarled, “What are you doing in Kearney? How did you get here?”

The lad calling himself Tanner replied, I worked a few days running errands for Miss Alaina Christiansen. Mostly I got here by walking.”

The judge snarled, “Because of your fighting, you were put in jail; because of your recalcitrance, I remanded you to jail…”

The lad smiled and interrupted, “Sir. At no time did I resist. I was not stubborn or the least bit obdurate in any way.”

The judge sat up and just stared; for a moment he was speechless, wondering how the lad dressed like a street urchin understood what he was saying, much less respond in a manner that the judge didn’t fully understand. After a long moment of confusion and thought, the judge changed the subject and again snapped, “Don’t be interrupting!”

The lad named Tanner had a slight smile; he nodded his head and said, “Yes, sir.”

Again, the judge glared at him; the response confused the judge; the lad was disturbing; after all, he had broken his son’s nose. Then the judge thought, in all his time in Kearney, he didn’t know of an Alaina Christianson. He looked to the bailiff, “Who the devil is this Miss Alaina Christianson?”

The bailiff asked, “May I approach the bench?”

The judge impatiently waved him forward. The bailiff explained, "Miss Alaina Christensen is the lady I spoke to you about. She thinks the boy is a real good lad, and she wanted to make sure I told you so. She also saw the fight from the very beginning, and she said it was your son that egged the boy on. She said it was as the boy explained: when your son ripped his shirt, only then did he fight back. Like the boy said, he popped your son in the nose; that was the end of it."

The judge thought he knew everyone in town; he asked, "Where does she live?"

"Right next to, 'what's her name.' Miss Christianson has been in town here only for a week."

The "What's her name" was code for one Beatrice Langley, a gal who had frequent visitors in the night. The judge's eyebrows raised a bit; he asked, "What does she look like?"

The bailiff shrugged, "I would say short, dark brown hair. Good-looking lady."

"What business is she in?"

"She's not in the Beatrice Langley game. She's an upright lady."

The judge's eyes seemed to open a bit wider at the description. "Alright, alright, alright, let's get done with this."

The bailiff was puzzled; the judge scowled at the information; it almost seemed like he didn't like the advice or the opinion of Alaina Christianson for some reason or other. The bailiff clarified, "She just wanted to make sure the information was a part of the record."

The judge nodded and repeated, "Alright, alright, alright, I heard you."

The judge shooed the bailiff away from the bench; he clenched his jaws and decided on a very quick fix to the situation. "Bailiff, keep him in chains and escort him to the railroad. The town will pay for his boarding passage as far as Denver. I want him out of town on the next train."

The judge rapped his gavel, got up, and left the room. Then suddenly the judge returned and ordered, "Bailiff. When you see him onto the train, come back here."

Tanner felt lucky; he figured he was getting a free passage to Denver, and he wasn't questioned about his origin. He was happy he didn't have to divulge his time as an indenture. Since his indenture wasn't quite over, he figured the judge may send him back to St. Louis.

The bailiff led Tanner down the street to the rail station in handcuffs as directed. The bailiff chuckled, "That kid of the judge needed his nose broken; maybe now he'll behave himself. Alaina told me that you were a quiet and very nice boy. If that is worth anything."

Tanner smiled, "I felt safe around Alaina. I appreciate her kindness. I do wish the judge's son was leaving instead of me. But that would mean the judge would still be around."

The bailiff chuckled at the joke and then asked, "So, I take it you don't have parents still alive?"

Tanner figured that the bailiff must have talked to Alaina; he shook his head, "No. I think maybe my mum maybe could have died in childbirth, twins; I think I somehow lived."

"Who brought you up?"

"Orphanage. First I was adopted; like I said, the parents maybe died of a sickness. If that's so, somehow I didn't get it. Not sure, but… one of the Mister's told me I may have been sold early on. I guess there were all sorts of stories. Somehow I got back to the orphanage when I was about three. When I was ten, I got a bit bigger; I was put on a farm, and then I think they got sick, or sick of me, and sold me to a shop owner in St. Louis as an indenture."

The bailiff shook his head. "That's against the law; they can't do that."

Tanner laughed, "Right before I ran away, I was about to be sold again; that's when I took off… I ran away."

Tanner smiled, "Now, the good judge gave me a free ride to Denver on the railroad. All I had to do was break his son's nose."

The bailiff laughed, "I've got to ask you, when you spoke up in front of the judge, exactly what did you say?"

Tanner chuckled and explained, "One of the Mister's at the orphanage liked to give us talks. He liked recalcitrance. We soon learned it meant stubborn, resistant, obstinate, and obdurate. I wanted to laugh when he used it on me."

The bailiff again chuckled, "Tanner, I know it will be hard but keep finding ways to smile. Sometimes we must look for humor where it doesn't seem humor can be found."

Tanner grinned and replied, "Thanks. Tell Alaina thanks for me. She's a good person."

The train was chugging into the station; the bailiff removed the handcuffs and said, "I wish you great luck in Denver. Try to stay out of fights with the judge's son, Mr. Freeman?"

As Tanner stepped onto the train, he turned, smiled, and said to the bailiff, "About having reasons to seek a bit of humor. My last name is Randolph. I told the judge my name was free man mainly to be funny. I've got a few months left of an indenture in St. Louis. My biggest fear was being sent back. Thanks again."

The bailiff chuckled, "The man you were indentured to; he treated you pretty rough?"

"Yes, sir. Then the guy he sold me to, he said he was going to keep me working in his factory well past when my indenture was over for no pay."

Before Tanner entered the train, the bailiff shook his hand. "Tanner Randolph, you can think on your feet. I think you will do alright. Find a job as quickly as you can when you get to Denver."

Tanner hesitated, then said, "I thank you for your smile. To an orphan, many times a smile is worth a lot."

The bailiff stood looking as the train pulled out; he thought that for many orphaned kids, a smile was perhaps a rare thing. Tanner's remark gave the bailiff a lot to consider. Whenever he dealt with people, he tried to be fair. In the place of dealing with an orphan, he could understand that a smile, a sign of acceptance, would be a mighty good thing.

The bailiff walked to the courthouse to report back to the judge. He felt good; even his step seemed a bit lighter. He was determined to earn Tanner's compliment.

The bailiff wondered why he was asked to return to the courtroom; all hearings scheduled for the day were over. The bailiff rapped on the door to the judge's chambers. After asking who it was, the judge opened the door.

The judge went to his desk and asked the bailiff to take a seat. The bailiff wondered what was happening; being alone with the judge was a first.

The judge wrote a few notes on a piece of paper, dried the ink, then slipped the note into a drawer. The judge then asked, "When is the next train for Denver due to depart?"

The bailiff answered, "Around noon tomorrow."

The judge ordered, "Tomorrow at eleven AM you will escort Alaina Christianson to the railroad depot. The city will pay her fare as far as Denver."

The bailiff was baffled; the woman was being chased out of town, and the judge has given no reason why.

Denver arrival. Monday June 2, 1879 late afternoon,

Mary Jane Tremble just happened to be walking by the Denver rail station when the train came in. It was Monday; she thought there would be no Orphan Train children on this day. As she walked by the station, a boy her age stepped around the side of the building, appearing almost like he was partially hiding, peering out at the street. He had tattered clothing on; he had all the earmarks of an orphan.

He stood looking about as though he didn't have a clue as to where he was going. There was plenty of traffic about; he had all sorts of men to get information from, and instead he just looked about, studying his surroundings.

Mary Jane watched with interest; she thought she understood him. As he walked slowly up the street, she followed a few steps behind; his eyes took in everything but swept past her; probably she wasn't a perceived threat. She smiled at her thoughts; she had been in his shoes once herself.

After a block she hurried a bit and caught up with him, determined to give him some help. "Hi. I'm Mary Jane Tremble. You look new to Denver; can I help?"

Mary Jane noted his face expressed a quizzical look; he had a very slight smile, and he hesitated to answer, obviously unsure of himself. Finally, he quietly answered, "I am looking for work."

Mary Jane thought that if it weren't for his clothing, he could get work just about anywhere in Denver. He did look like an orphan, a badly mistreated one at that. Mary Jane asked, "Maybe I can help. Do you have a preference for work? Do you have any experience?"

The boy slowly nodded his head, measuring his words. Mary Jane could see that he wondered if he should be talking to her at all. His quiet demeanor told her much about his character; he wouldn't make any brash moves or statements; he was in a self-protective mode; one she recalled in her past.

The boy slowly nodded, "I worked with farming; I worked with wood and a bit with metal, blacksmithing."

Mary Jane asked, "What is your name?"

The boy smiled, "Tanner."

Mary Jane replied, "Tanner. I will take you to a blacksmith just up the street. The rest is up to you."

Again, Tanner smiled; he wondered what possessed her to assist him. Tanner replied, "Thank you for your help, Mary Jane Tremble."

Tanner figured that, as an orphan, he was usually ignored or sent away; this girl went out of her way to approach him. He wondered why.

On the way to the blacksmith shop, she decided to come right out and ask, "Can I ask you where you are from?"

Tanner had a bigger smile now; he felt good that she wanted to know more about him and wondered why in the world she was interested in him at all. He decided to blurt the truth. He told about his indenture, getting away, traveling to Kearney, punching the judge's son in the nose, and being jailed. He told about the judge's ruling and being put on the train as far as Denver.

Mary Jane considered that as an indenture, two or more times sold, he was a person who had been mistreated at every turn yet spoke without malice. He even joked about his bad luck rather than blaming the judge in the latest occurrence.

Mary Jane took him right to the door of the blacksmith shop. "The owner's name is Goran Burkhart. Good luck to you, Tanner."

As Mary Jane walked away, she fully understood what she was doing. Leaving him there, she understood that he may not follow through with the job. She knew that he may well seek out something with less confrontation. If there was less need to talk and therefore less chance of being turned away, less chance of rejection: that was the learned nature of orphans.

She thought of the saying, “You can lead a horse to water, but you can’t make him drink.”

There were traits she liked in Tanner; she thought he may have the strength of character to pursue a steady job. In the case of many orphans, they fear reaching out, exposing who they are and what they stand for. They simply have had too much experience with rejection and outright abuse.

Mary Jane Tremble smiled; she recalled her struggle with being ignored and abused as a ten-year-old. She smiled. She thought when she returned home, she would have to give her adoptive mother a warm hug.

Kearney, Nebraska. Tuesday, June 3, 1879

At a little past 10:30, the bailiff knocked on the door of Alaina Christianson. The bailiff had seen her a couple of times about town, but other than that, he knew nothing about her. When she opened the door, she smiled and said, "Mr. Thompson. How are you today?"

In most of his dealings with anyone connected to the courts, he was simply the bailiff. He wondered how she got his name. He responded, "Alaina, I'm sorry to say, I'm here as a court official. I've been asked to put you on the noon train to Denver. The city will pay your fee."

Alaina was puzzled; she crossed her arms, smiled, and guessed, "Did the good judge, Mr. Odell Swinton, order this?"

"Yes, ma'am."

Alaina smiled, "And if I don't want to go?"

The bailiff shrugged, "My orders are to put you on the train. I'm not paid to wrestle with anyone."

Alaina was relaxed, as if this wasn't really a bother at all. "Mr. Thompson, I'm sure you'd win the wrestling match, but I surely would like to know: What is the reason I'm being expelled?"

"I don't know."

"Would you run and ask, please? There is plenty of time to get on to the train. I'll pack when you are gone."

John Thompson smiled; he wondered the same thing; now she gave him an excuse to ask. He decided he liked her attitude; to him, it showed Alaina to possess a curious inner strength.

Alaina was packed when the bailiff returned. She asked, "What did the good judge say?"

"He did a bit of yelling and said something about being indigent."

"Goodness. The judge knows nothing about me. What evidence did he provide?"

The bailiff smiled and shook his head. "He said if I couldn't get the job done, he'd get the deputy."

Alaina laughed, "Mr. Thompson, for the most part I like Kearney, but there is little here that holds me. As a matter of fact, I was thinking of moving on to Denver. Help me carry my luggage. We should be able to make it to the station on time."

When Alaina picked up her purse, she slipped a pistol inside. John Thompson grinned and asked, "Is that a five-shot Remington Rider?"

Alaina nodded, "Why yes. You are knowledgeable about weapons."

The bailiff smiled, "Yes. I've read about the Rider. It's quite a weapon for such a small thing. Five shots,. .32 caliber at close range, my goodness. How did you come by one? I understand they are fairly costly.

Alaina laughed and said, "Mr. Thompson, surely you know that every indigent lady carries one?"

John Thompson laughed; there was much more to Alaina than the good judge understood. He replied, "I think the judge bit off a bit more than he should chew."

While waiting at the station, Alaina said, "So the good judge doesn't like it when you question him?"

The bailiff nodded, "That's very correct. He does get mighty upset."

"Well Mr. Thompson, I'll tell you why the good judge is shooing me out of his little town. I've only been here a week, and I've met the judge two times. Once when he was coming from, and once when he was going to, Ms. Beatrice Langley's boudoir. I believe all the townspeople refer to her as, 'What's her name?' Do you think the good judge is merely trying to get rid of an eyewitness to his philandering?"

The bailiff chuckled; although she was in town for a short time, she had good knowledge of what was going on. "When I mentioned your name and where you were staying in Tanner Randolph's brief trial, he did have a mighty big scowl on his face. At the time I wondered what that was all about."

Alaina asked, "Given Tanner's background, he is a very nice young lad. What did the judge do with Tanner?"

The bailiff explained how the judge demanded that Tanner be locked up for the weekend and then summarily sent to the train in handcuffs. Even the bailiff thought the treatment was excessive, and the sheriff who put Tanner in jail seemed apologetic.

Alaina asked, "The sheriff's name is Jim?"

"Yes. Jim Larson."

The train pulled into the station, and the bailiff helped Alaina load her luggage onto the train. When she was settled in, she said, "Thank you, Mr. Thompson. Please tell the judge that since he seemed to be interested in my whereabouts, I will write. Tell him he may not like what I write or where the writing ends up, but please tell him that I will write."

Question of origin
Tuesday, June 3, 1879

In the library of the spacious Denver home of recently deceased Randolph and Mary Kristofferson, their son Randolph was trying to gather information about his past. The freaky landslide that killed his parents just three weeks earlier left Randolph with a myriad of questions he had been looking forward to getting an answer to.

Randolph asked, “Tell me, Uncle Edmund, exactly how… What were the circumstances of my adoption?”

It was a point-blank question that his mother and father never answered before they died in that landslide. They had promised to tell him before he turned 18. Randolph Kristofferson IV just inherited his parents’ entire fortune, and somehow his uncle was quickly appointed as his guardian and the estate’s executor.

For some unknown reason, confusing to Randolph, at nearly 18 years old, he was not involved in the court hearing that gave his uncle Edmond charge of his father and mother’s estate. It was more confusing because Eddie was never a part of their lives, and some time earlier, his father told him his brother Eddie wasn’t the most trustworthy sort, and he should give thought to what isn’t being said when talking to Eddie.

His uncle looked up from sorting through his papers and slowly answered, “You knew you were adopted?”

So typical of his uncle, Randolph thought, asking a question of a question.

Randolph nodded, “Yes. Dad promised to tell me everything before I turned 18. Now I suppose it’s up to you.”

Edmond stared out the window at the mountains and was obviously deep in thought. He waited so long to reply that Randolph was reminded again of his father’s admonition, “With Eddie, give thought to what isn’t being said.”

Finally, Eddie replied, “My brother and Mary couldn’t have kids. He wanted the family name to go on. You were lucky.”

Getting a bit impatient, Randolph changed how he addressed his uncle, “I know I was lucky. So, Eddie, where was I when I was adopted? What were the circumstances of the adoption? Did Mom and Dad know my birth mother and father?”

There was silence as Eddie thought and slowly shook his head. Finally, he spoke in circles, divulging nothing: “There were thousands of kids on the streets, in orphanages; people were even selling their kids because they couldn’t take care of them.”

Randolph wondered what it would take to get a straight answer out of Eddie. He repeated the question, “Did they know my mother?”

Eddie slowly shook his head as if weighing his options rather than thinking about answering the question, “I don’t think so. I’m not certain. I just think they got you from an orphanage someplace.”

Again, Randolph thought Eddie was intentionally vague; Randolph already knew he was from an orphanage. Did Eddie know more? If he knew more details, why wouldn’t he share them? Randolph knew the court tied him to Eddie until he was 18, less than four months from now.

Randolph pushed for information , “Eddie, you can’t even recall the city?”

Even at the near insult, Eddie slowly shook his head; Randolph’s father’s words came back to him again: Eddie isn’t the most trustworthy sort, and one must give thought to what isn’t being said when talking to Eddie.

Frustrated and disgusted, sure that he wasn’t going to get a reliable answer, Randolph got up and said, “I’m going down to the bank for a bit.”

Randolph began wondering what, if anything, Eddie stood to gain by withholding information. Randolph could see by the scowl on Eddie’s face that even going to the bank his father owned and ran was or could be problematic.

At the bank Randolph Kristofferson went directly to his father's office; the door was locked. He went to the teller, "Miriam, could you give me the key to my father's office?"

Miriam thought nothing out of the ordinary; she gave Randolph the key. For the next few hours, he went through his father's files; that mostly involved the business of the bank. If there was any question, he ignored the file completely. Choosing only to investigate family related files.

Toward the back of the drawer, he found one with memorabilia, mostly notes and cards that he had given to his father. A typical keepsake file, many were childish drawings he could not recall, and a few brought back fond memories and elicited tears.

Francis Greer knocked and entered the office. Apologetically he said, "Your Uncle Edward indicated that we should keep this door locked."

"I agree. I'll lock it when I leave."

Francis now a bit awkwardly explained, "Actually, Edward indicated that we should not allow you to even enter the office."

Randolph was sitting at his father's desk. He thought for a moment; at home, Eddie locked his father's office and kept him from entering under the pretense of preserving papers, and now the same directive existed for him at his father's office in the bank.

Randolph grinned; he read the paper in his hand to Francis, "Francis, I can see why Uncle Eddie would want to keep me from seeing this. This is a letter from me to Father when I was six years old: Dear Daddy. Thank you for the bicycle. I love you. Randy. I confess, Francis, I spelled bicycle wrong."

Randolph shook his head and asked, "Francis. I'm wondering why you were told to keep me out of here. Did Eddie explain?"

Francis sat down, obviously in deep thought; he knew within a very few months Randolph would be the owner and his boss. He slowly shook his head, "No. He just said he was appointed by the judge as executor of the estate. It is confusing. Randolph, you've been to this office a thousand times. I know that you know, understand, and protect the sanctity of every document, every file."

Randolph nodded, "Yes. A lot better than Uncle Eddie. Francis, you've been with my father for a long time. Does Eddie have a key to this office? And has he been in here?"

Francis nodded, "He has a key, but so far he has not been in here."

Randolph thought for some time, "Francis. I want you to get Rudy in here today and change the locks on my father's office door." He hesitated for a minute and then added, "Have Rudy have three keys available. For now, one will be locked in the safe. You will have one, and I will have one. Eddie will not be allowed in this office. We'll do this under the pretense of protecting the customer's information."

Francis smiled; his first objective would be to protect the bank and all its records. Francis nodded, "Very good. I'll see to it immediately."

Randolph added, "If I remove anything from this office," Randolph held up the paper he had just read, "including my notes to father when I was six years old, I'll clear it with you. Also, until I turn eighteen years old, I will not delve into any files that pertain to the bank; if there is a question as to what the file pertains to, I won't open the file."

Randolph's mind seemed to awaken a bit after his father's and mother's untimely and sudden death. He wondered why he was being kept out of his own father's home office. He had been in and out of both offices' countless times. What could the reason be?

Randolph thought about the home office; he wondered what Eddie needed in either office. He said to Francis, "When Rudy gets done here, send him to the house. I'm going to have him change the lock on my father's office at home also. If Uncle Eddie needs to get in the office for something specific, he can do it with me present and explain why it is necessary."

Edward Kristofferson, known to most in his circle of friends as Eddie, watched as Randolph walked into the bank; he didn't know if the kid could learn anything at the bank; he didn't even know if it would matter, but it bothered him. He nervously thought Mildred may be angry with him for letting Randolph have access to his father's office.

He was into this way over his head, and he wondered how he ever got involved in the first place. Drunk or not, why did he go along with it in the first place? Mildred may be able to soothe his nerves; besides, it was getting late in the day, and he could use a drink.

He put his hat on and walked out the door; he felt overdue for a stiff drink and he missed putting his elbows on the bar at the Goldstrike Saloon. As he entered the saloon he recalled that under orders from Mildred, he had been staying away since the death of his brother and sister-in-law. The more he thought about the whole deal, the more he needed that drink. A quick drink, then he'd go up and report to Mildred.

As he entered the saloon, he thought that before all this he liked coming in here for a drink and a quick visit with Mildred. At the bar he ordered a beer and a shot of whiskey. He tossed down the shot of whiskey; ordering another one was automatic.

As he sipped his beer, he thought there would be some hissing going on when he got to Mildred's room. She didn't want to see him now, and she didn't like him drinking while this entire mess was going on. The whiskey seemed to calm his nerves; Eddie grinned; he thought that lately Mildred found a whole lot to hiss about.

With a couple of shots and a beer in him, he asked the bartender, "Mildred in?"

Bill Snider, the bartender and owner, smirked, "She's busy. Should be done shortly."

Eddie shrugged; he tried to hide the fact that he was now mad. She told him he was done taking in customers. "Give me another shot."

Bill smiled knowingly. "How are things going at the Kristofferson palace?"

Eddie wondered what he should say, he wondered exactly how much the bartender knew. Nervous, he decided to stay quiet; he shrugged without answering.

Eddie nursed this shot; hell, he wanted to get drunk, and he found enough money in his brother's desk drawer to get drunk and stay that way for a month or two, but he had to play his cards right. The whiskey loosened his tongue; liquor always made him talk. He couldn't drink so much that he'd talk.

Another ten minutes and the bartender spoke quietly to him, "Eddie, it's your turn."

Eddie was insulted by the remark, but he tilted the empty shot glass and then downed the remainder of the beer before wavering to the stairway. He made his way to Mildred's room, knocked on the door, and opened it. Mildred was tidying up at her washstand.

The walls were paper thin, and as predicted, she hissed, "I thought I told you to stay away for a while. Did you find the deed to the mine?"

Eddie's head bobbed from side to side; he was way over his head, and now the whiskey wasn't helping him think. He whispered, "Still haven't found the title. I need some advice… the kid went to the bank."

Mildred hissed, "Damn. Why the hell did you allow him to go there?"

Eddie snapped back at a whisper, "He owns the damn bank. He'll soon take over. He's been going there for years. What the hell can I do?"

Trying to gain a bit of the high ground, Eddie hastened to add, "I thought you said you were done taking in customers?"

Since Eddie had the guts to ask the question, it served only to light Mildred's fire, "Hell. You are damn near drunk. Now what the hell did you tell the bartender?"

Eddie shook his head. "Nuthin'!"

Mildred ordered, "Sit down!"

Eddie thought another damn lecture was coming. He sat down, but he fired back, “I don’t know how or why I let you talk me into this.”

Mildred got in his face and hissed, “Dammit! We are in this together. We’ll hang together if we get caught. If we pull this off, we’ll cash in and head to Europe and live like royalty.”

Eddie hung his head; he figured it was the same damn story. How the hell did he get talked into doing away with his own brother and his brother’s wife? Hell, he didn’t give a damn about running away to Europe. He wondered how much whiskey they made there.

Seeing that he was in a world of his own, Mildred cuffed him on the cheek and hissed, “Damn, you’re not listening again. How much did you have to drink?”

Eddie got up to go, “I came here to get some advice, not to get the hell beat out of me.”

Eddie started for the door; Mildred grabbed him, sensing that she had gone too far. “Eddie. Where are you going?”

Eddie pulled away and opened the door. “Back to the house. I’m going to take a nap.”

Eddie had a bottle in the house; usually he would lock himself in his room so he could drink all by himself.

Mildred went to powder her nose; she had to have a long talk with the bartender.

Denver
Tues. June 3, late afternoon

Alaina wasn't shocked at her treatment by the courts, the people at the rail station, or on the train; even the porters seemed standoffish. A woman traveling alone seemed always to be placed in a very dishonorable category. After an hour of shopping around and asking questions, she was able to rent a buggy with a recommended driver to show her about the town.

The name given to her was Arvid. When the buggy arrived, she stood by her luggage. "Arvid?"

"Yes, ma'am."

He got down to help her with her bags. Alaina asked, "What are your usual fees, Arvid?"

"A half dollar will get you a tour of the entire town, then any place in Denver."

"Arvid. You have been recommended to me. I'm going to give you two dollars. For the two dollars, I would like the tour, some information, and most importantly, an agreement not to divulge any of our conversation to anyone as long as I am in town. Can you agree to that?"

Arvid nodded and smiled; he was making about three days' worth of wages at his usual rate. "Yes, ma'am. I can do that."

"You can call me Alaina."

Arvid loaded her bags and asked, "Where are we off to?"

Alaina explained, "I want a place to stay where I can get a flavor of perhaps the, ahhh… less fortunate side of your fair city."

Arvid asked, "Hotel?"

"Not necessarily. A place where I can lock the door and perhaps have a bit of privacy and still be able to observe the ahh… unfortunate…"

They were a mile or so from the railroad station when Arvid stopped the buggy. Without pointing, he explained, "Alaina.

Here you have a bit of everything our little town has to offer, from the very bottom to the very top. See the big house up the street on the left? That's a piece of the top of Denver. It is the Kristofferson home. Both Randolph and his wife Mary were killed in a strange accident here less than a month ago. From what I understand, there was a freak landslide when they were on the way to their mine. The bank up the street on the left is also a property of their estate."

Alaina wondered out loud, "I wonder, with their palatial home and a bank, what they were doing at a mine?"

"A lot of people asked the same question. From what I've heard, they just decided to take a drive out to look at the mine."

Intuitively, Alaina inquired, "How many owners were there?"

"Not sure; the judge was a part owner, not sure how big a part."

Alaina bristled a bit at the recollection of her treatment from the Kearney judge, Odell Swinton. She asked, "Who all inherits the mine and the bank?"

"Not exactly certain. From what I've heard, there is just a young lad. He was usually in close company with his mother and father; I don't know why he wasn't with them on the trip to the mine."

"What's the boy's name?"

"Not sure, maybe Randolph."

"Now Arvid, where do you recommend I stay?"

Arvid nodded to the right and replied, "If you want to experience the bottom of the barrel. The Goldstrike Saloon has rooms upstairs. There are a couple of ladies there that share their rooms; they are at the bottom of that barrel. The reason I mention the place is that there is a back stair that is locked. I understand you can get in and out without stepping in the bar or even being seen by that crowd. I also understand there are good working locks on the doors."

Arvid smiled. "Still, I have to ask you, just in case, what kind of protection you have."

Alaina patted her purse. "I have insurance. A five-shot Remington Rider in which I am proficient, but I am also very cautious. Now Arvid, what about the cost of rent for a month?"

Arvid asked, "Do you want me to ask the owner if anything is available?"

"Please negotiate for me. I would also be concerned about toiletry and access to fresh water. If the cost is less than ten dollars a month, then I will accept."

Arvid was back shortly; he handed her two keys. He explained, "The bigger key is to the back door. The smaller brass key is for room three. There is an outdoor toilet in the back; the larger key fits that toilet also. It is to be used only by the three renters."

Arvid assured, "I checked; there is water right outside your door. You have containers in your room; take whatever you need. The cost per month is seven dollars."

Alaina handed Arvid a ten-dollar bill. "Arvid. I got a much better deal than I bargained for. Pay the owner and keep the extra."

They drove around the back of the saloon and used the back stairway. Once settled with her bags in the room, she said, "Thank you, Arvid. Remember our agreement."

Arvid smiled, "Yes, Alaina. Mum's the word. If you have need for a ride, drop a note at the counter of the café just down the street. I usually end up eating there in the morning, and I try to go by the rail station about three or four in the afternoon when the train arrives."

Once the door was closed, Alaina took out her writing tablet.

Mr. Joseph Pulitzer, the, New York World.

Joseph. I am in Denver; you may edit and print this article when you wish. I perceive no physical danger to me from the release of the article.

Tuesday June 3, 1879

This morning I was given an hour's notice to get out of the little town of Kearney, Nebraska. When I asked the bailiff delivering the message why I was being forced to leave, he did not know. I sent him back to the good judge, Mr. Odell Swinton, to inquire. Judge Swinton indicated that I was 'indigent.' (Be sure to tell my father that I have become 'indigent.' Father will be amused.)

I believe the reason the judge asked me to leave was because, on two occasions, I met the judge entering one night and leaving another night, the boudoir of one of the 'ladies of the night.' As a matter of fact, I have learned; the town refers to her as, 'What's her name.'

The good judge was no doubt attempting to spare himself some embarrassment by shooing me out of town. I told the judge I would write. Now, I'm sure that the judge's embarrassment will be much more multiplied.

I feel the judge also needs official condemnation. His decision in my case, and in the case of an orphan lad, is deserving of peer rebuke.

On Monday, June 2, 1879, Judge Swinton sent an orphan boy out of town for protecting himself against the judge's son. I observed the altercation. The orphan was verbally and physically attacked because of his clothing. Only after the judge's son intentionally ripped the pocket on the orphan's shirt did the orphan finally defend himself with a single blow to the nose of the aggressor.

I witnessed the entire thing. For defending himself, the judge had the orphan spend the weekend in jail and was then made to go to court in handcuffs. After the court hearing, the bailiff was ordered to deliver the orphan to the rail station and then put him on the train. Only then was the bailiff allowed to remove the handcuffs from the totally compliant young man.

In both cases, I believe the judge acted inappropriately with no regard for the law or fair play.

Yours to seek a just world,
Annie in Hiding.

The note to the New York World newspaper completed, Alaina put a glass on the wall and listened briefly when there was an obvious rhythmic creaking of the bed in the next room. She quietly unpacked and busied herself checking her bed for bedbugs. Finding none, she prepared and disguised her writing materials and any record of her being connected to a newspaper.

The door opened and closed next door; the walls were thin, and she could hear someone washing, a glass being bumped, then a bit later footsteps, the door opening again and closing. Alaina thought her neighbor was a busy gal.

Alaina put the glass to the wall and listened for any nefarious chatter. To be prepared, her pencil and paper were ready.

The high-pitched sound of a female's excited voice was barely heard, "I thought I… you to stay away…"

Him. ...find... deed…?

Her. "Why the hell…"

Him. "went to bank… What the hell can I do?"

Him. "I thought you were done taking customers."

Her. "Hell… drunk… What did you tell the bartender?"

Him. "Nuthin."

Her. "Sit down."

Him. "I don't know why… I let you talk to me like that."

Her. "Damn it! We are in this together. We'll hang… go to Europe and live like royalty."

Her. "Damn. Not listening… much drink?"

Him. "I came for advice… get beat up…"

Her. "Eddie. Where are you going?"

Him. "Back to the house… take a nap."

Alaina put the glass and her pencil down and waited till she heard the neighbor's door open and close. She figured the gal left and went down the stairway into the saloon. She hid or disguised all of her writing materials; it was now a little past 6 o'clock. Alaina decided it was time to dine; Arvid indicated there was a café just a half block away.

In her travels Alaina had developed a nose for news. She sought out conflict, she wrote articles about fair play, and she exposed favoritism and crooked dealing. The words of the woman next door came to her, "We'll hang…" Then, "Europe… live like royalty."

The 'we'… they did something so wrong the punishment would be hanging. We… how big a number is the 'we' part? Just the two of them, or was there more… If they get away with it, they'll live in Europe like royalty. That sounded like just two people. Or would they separate from others?

Alaina mused, 'Eddie,' it will be easy to find out the woman's name since she was living right next door through a paper-thin wall. She continued to go over the talk, enhancing her notes where she recalled what was said. She kept going over the possibility of hanging. There was also obvious discord among the thieves.

She whispered to herself, "What a way to start my first day in Denver?!"

Alaina quietly slipped out the door, made sure it was locked, then placed a tiny piece of paper about an inch below the brass of the door jamb. If the paper was not there upon her return, she would have to enter the saloon and talk to the owner.

The café had a counter and a harvest table; the harvest table easily sat ten, and there were six others already seated. Usually, she would sit at the counter and pump the waitress or the cook for information; today she sat at the harvest table where she would benefit from the conversation.

Alaina took a seat; she noted that one of the men had a copy of the New York World newspaper. Upon closer inspection, she noted the paper was a familiar addition. She thought she would have to write a letter to the editor, Joseph Pulitzer, and speak of the Denver circulation.

The fare this day was a stew, a generous serving with plenty of vegetables; meanwhile, the one reading the paper spoke up and related, "I love to read this gal's articles."

A guy with an out-of-place derby hat asked, "Who is that? What does she write about?"

"She goes by the name of "Annie in Hiding. She likes to expose people who are doing some pretty bad things. This article is about a place in St. Louis that is running a bawdy house."

The derby hat shrugged, "Heck, we have our own bawdy house ladies right here in Denver."

"This article exposed a guy that traps young gals that he uses in his bawdy house."

The Derby hat ordered, "Just read the article, Joe. Bob here can't read, and I'll eat while you read. Do you ladies mind?"

One of the ladies replied, "I've already read the article, so go right ahead. They got what they deserved."

Joe started, "The article was written in early March of this year, but it is hard to know when Annie in Hiding actually did the investigation."

The Derby hat asked, "Why don't they tell us the date?"

Joe shook his head. "Because she is in hiding. She doesn't want anyone to know who she is. She could get herself killed for something like this if they found her identity.

"So, the article reads:" 'When arriving in St. Louis, I took a buggy tour of the city; my idea was to search for a problem that needs to be addressed by all of us. The second day I concentrated my search not far from the railroad station after hearing a rumor that men were taking very young ladies off from the Orphan Train and using them in houses of prostitution. I was in complete disbelief; I had to investigate.

After some casual inspection of the two houses mentioned, I discovered that a problem in dire need of a solution existed.

An informer indicated that the girls were purchased for anywhere from twenty-five to fifty dollars. Someone, sometimes a customer, would sign up for a girl on the Orphan Train supposedly as an indenture and then sell the girl to the bawdy house. Having heard of the going price, I struck on a plan.

The rumor was that one 'house' had at least twelve girls, and they seemed to operate with impunity. Under the pretense of purchasing a maid for my house, I entered. In order not to be preyed upon myself, I acted as the part of one privileged, as if I expected to be listened to; I put on an air of imperiousness.

I asked to see the girls available to be purchased. When only one was brought out, I demanded to see them all. I got away with the act. I think, when I showed the owner, one Wilbert Stevens, a handful of cash, the agreement was quick and simple.

There were no documents for the transaction, of course nothing that would provide evidence of money changing hands. For fifty dollars I 'purchased' Milly, mostly because she was a very frightened young lady who I soon learned was just fourteen years old.

When the girls were brought out for me to select, most of them put on a 'good face.' I think that even if they were not knowing what they were getting into, they wanted to get away.

I took Milly to my hotel room and quietly explained what I was doing. After assuring her several times over that she would never go back to Mr. Stevens. I explained that I would enlist the help of some very influential people to put Mr. Stevens and his cadre of people preying on young girls out of business. I explained that more than likely he and his cohorts would be in jail; Milly was very happy; she cried.

Milly gave me this story: Most of the girls indeed were taken off the Orphan Train by customers or friends of Mr. Stevens. They would sign for possession of the girl, and then they would sell them to Stevens.

I asked Milly, "Don't the people from the Orphan Train check up on the girls?"

Sadly, the girls could easily be reported as running away, and then nobody would check up on them.

If indeed they did run away or sneak out of the bawdy house, if caught they were very badly beaten. The memory was fresh for Milly; she cried again.

All the girls felt trapped. I asked if indeed they were used for sex. Milly nodded and cried. I asked their ages; she indicated the youngest was twelve, the oldest was seventeen.

I asked what happened when the girls were pregnant. Milly told the story of Luann; they took her away for the day and brought her back late that night. Luann died in the night; the details I cannot bear to share.

Readers: children cannot be used this way. Mr. Wilbert Stevens and every one of his ilk needs to be put out of business; in his case, tried for murder. Also, the people who took the girls off the Orphan Train need to be held to account, fined, jailed, or my solution would start with a very good horsewhipping.

The people of the Orphan Train need to aggressively check up on these very vulnerable girls.

What about Milly? (Not her real name.)

Milly is doing fine right now in the home of good friends, where their daily task is to give Milly something to smile about while providing her with the best education and everything she needs to be proud of herself, to be a success in her own eyes.

Joe shook his head and said, "This is the best part. I'll give you the short of the investigation. Milly happily gave the authorities of the Child Services nearly all the proper names of the girls, also those names she recalled of the ones selling the favors of the girls, and names of girls purchased never to return. Armed with Milly's information and a gentle push from Annie in Hiding, the New York World newspaper sent reporters to St. Louis.

"Over fifteen people are in jail in St. Louis with every conceivable charge imaginable, from rape, selling children, and child slavery to murder.

"As Annie in Hiding said in the beginning of this article, this is a problem all of us must put an end to. She is right; we can't look the other way."

Joe got up to go, "I'm running late. The article goes into greater depth about the situation; they name names, and the sheriff in St. Louis has added one remark I'd like to read. He said, "I would really like to administer Annie in Hiding's horsewhipping punishment, but I doubt if the court will allow me to do that."

As Joe walked away, he laughed, "After reading this paper, I hope Annie in Hiding is feeling good right now."

Alaina smiled as she ate her stew; she would have more to tell the editor.

Conspiracy
Wednesday June 4, 1879.
Late morning

Eddy woke up with a screaming headache; at first he wondered where he was, then it all came back to him. He was in a room at his brother's house; he was in league with Mildred; he helped get his own brother killed. Damn, he was drunk when he agreed to send his brother to the mine.

Now, he had one main job to do: he had to get his hands on his brother's title to the mine so the judge could change it to his liking. Eddy shook his head; hell, he thought, he didn't tell Mildred that he stunk at reading, and he hated going through files, especially the ones written in longhand he found doubly hard to read.

This day was like the rest; he didn't know where to start. He thought he better get dressed and try to find that damn file with the deed to the mine.

When he got to the kitchen, the cook was there. Eddie asked, "Got something to nibble on?"

Art pointed, "There's a loaf of bread, got some butter, and a bit of apple butter. Lunch will be ready about 12:30; Rand said he'd be back about then."

Eddie cut a slice of bread and asked, "Where's Randolph off to?"

Art replied, "Went to the bank about eight this morning."

Eddie scowled; hell, he'll be in trouble again with Mildred. He ate the bread, had a cup of coffee, and decided he needed a good drink. He took the coffee and headed to the office to look for that damn title to the mine.

He wrestled with the door; he thought he had the wrong key. For ten minutes he tried in vain to open the door. He went back to the kitchen with the coffee cup, put it on the counter, and said, "Art. I can't seem to get into the office."

Art was at the stove; he stated, "Yeah. I saw Rudy here yesterday afternoon, sometime after you headed to the Goldstrike. I think Rudy was changing the lock."

Eddie barked, "Why didn't Rudy tell me? Where is the key?"

"If you were in your room, you didn't answer your door."

"Where's the key?"

"You will have to ask Rand; he had the locks changed."

"Why'd he do that?"

Art gave him an insulting look. "You are going to have to ask him. He'll be back here in another hour or two. With his dad and mom gone, he can do what he pleases. If you got a problem with that, talk to Rand."

Eddie was suddenly lost. He was near panic. He had to talk to Mildred. He practically ran down the street to the Goldstrike Saloon. By the time he got there, he decided he had to calm his nerves. He nervously tapped on the bar and ordered, "Give me a double."

The double shot of whiskey went down easily; he turned and started to the stairs. The bartender said, "Eddie. Where are you going?"

Eddie pointed up the stairs and kept going.

Alaina was in her room writing when she heard rapid footsteps up the stairs; then she heard a hurried knocking on the neighbor's door and a rattle when someone tried to shake the locked door.

After a few more nervous and impatient rattles of the doorknob, the door was opened. Alaina had her glass to the wall listening, but the glass wouldn't have been necessary. The occupant snapped, "What the hell are you doing here? I told you to stay away. You are going to get us hung."

"The kid had the locks changed. I can't get in the office."

"Damn it. And you didn't find the title yesterday?"

"Hell no." He didn't want to tell her that he didn't even try because he was too damn drunk.

"Hold your voice down. Where's the kid?"

"He's at the bank. He's been there since eight this morning."

"Damn Eddie, you are useless. Let me think."

Alaina's pencil was scribbling rapidly; now she noted the silence for a minute, and then she heard the order, "OK. Get back there and see if you can figure out why he changed the locks. That's important. We have to know what he's found. Does he know anything, especially about the title to the mine? Go!"

Alaina could hear the door open, and then she heard, "Don't talk about the title, and don't bring up the title."

"How am I going to find out about the title if I don't ask him?"

"Damn. If he brings up the subject, let him talk about it. Get out of here."

Alaina scribbled down a good part of the discussion while listening; she figured the gal was disenchanted with Eddie, her partner in crime.

Collusion feared.

Get us hung.

Eddie. Kid changed the locks.

Did Eddie find the title?

Eddie. No.

Where is the kid?

Eddie. At the bank since eight this morning.

Why did he change the locks?

What does the kid know? What did he find?

Does the kid know about the title to the mine?

Find the title…

Eddie. If I don't ask, how do I find out what he knows about the title?

Don't bring up the subject!

Alaina listened as her neighbor's door opened; she stepped to the stair rail and yelled down at the bartender, "Bill! We have to talk!"

Alaina heard steps on the stairway; she readied herself for whatever came her way; she shifted the opening of her purse slightly and slipped her hand in to make sure the handle of the .32 caliber Remington Rider was easily accessed. Then she went back to writing.

When the bartender entered the room next door, her neighbor spoke, "We are in deep crap."

"Wait a minute. Is Alyce in her room?"

"No. She's gone for the day."

"I have to check and see if there is anyone in number three."

Alaina's hand slipped into her purse and gripped the Remington Rider. A key rattled in her lock, and her homemade alarm noisily rattled as the door opened. As the bartender and owner stepped into her room, he was met with Alaina's pistol pointed at his chest.

Alaina yelled, "Who are you? What are you doing in my room?"

The pistol aimed at his chest was shocking; the racket of her homemade alarm and her loud voice further shook him. He finally spoke, "I own this place. I am your landlord."

Alaina picked up a megaphone and held it to her ear and yelled back at him, "What did you say?"

He spoke loudly, "I am your landlord."

Alaina again spoke loudly, "You are darn lucky you aren't dead, landlord. Knock and knock loudly the next time you need to come in here; don't come barging in here. And speak up so I can hear you."

The bartender looked down at the bells that jangled when he opened the door; the Remington Rider was still leveled at his chest. Alaina yelled, "What do you want?"

The bartender made up an excuse for being there. "I just wanted to know if you were alright."

Alaina answered, "I'm fine. But you were pretty damn near dead. Don't be scaring me again! I don't trust the trigger on this thing."

He noted that the gun was still leveled at his chest. He left shaking his head. Alaina released the hammer on the pistol, got up, and quickly locked the door. Upon returning to the desk, she put the glass against the wall and readied her pencil and paper.

Bill spoke, "She's damn near deaf. She damn near killed me. What the hell do you want, Mildred?"

"You're not going to believe what a dumb ass we've got tangled up with."

"Eddie? Now what?"

"Of course it's Eddie. The kid changed the locks on the door to the home office. Eddie can't get in. We are going to have to go to the judge and get an order to get in there."

"Damn. We can't go to the judge. That's out. Just wait. Eddie can search the bank office. The title could well be there. Just give this a few days. Don't get jumpy like Eddie. Without the title there will be nothing to show for our little accident."

"We are going to have to get rid of him; he's messing this whole thing up."

"You are talking like Eddie now. We can't get rid of him until this whole thing is settled. Remember, don't get jumpy. There's a lot of money at stake here. I'm going back to work. Just wait a few days…"

Alaina looked at her notepad.

Bar… She's damn near deaf—she damn near killed me.

Mildred... not believe what a dumb ass we got tangled up with.

Bar… Eddie?

Mildred. Yes. Kid changed the locks on the home office. Get the judge to order them to get in.

Bar… Damn, can't go to the judge! Wait. Eddie can search the bank for the title.

Mildred. Get rid of him! (Eddie?)

Bar… Agree—when settled, get the damn title first or we'll have nothing to show for our little accident.

Bar... a lot of money at stake.

Bar… (adamant!) Wait a few days!

Alaina thought the freak accident was not an accident. Mildred, the bartender, Bill, and Eddie, now she's going to have to learn about the 'kid. Who is the kid?'

Alaina thought she was going to have to get in touch with Arvid. She also figured that she would have to act as though she was very hard of hearing.

A Pedestal
Thursday, June 5, 1879.
Noon.

On the bench outside Goran Burkhart's blacksmith shop, Tanner was eating his lunch, Mary Jane Tremble timed her visit well. Usually Tanner's lunch break was about this time of day. Today Tanner was on the bench finishing his lunch; Mary Jane smiled as she boldly sat down beside him.

Tanner smiled. Mary Jane knew he liked her company but sensed he was still a little nervous; he looked down, smiled, and adjusted the tear in his shirt pocket. Mary Jane made small talk, "What's for lunch?"

Tanner was dressed in the same ill-fitting, worn, and dusty clothes. His shrug about his lunch then generous smile showed he was very pleased with her visit. Mary Jane asked, "Made up your mind yet?"

A moment's doubt as to her meaning showed, so she smiled and asked, "Are you going to the dance?"

Some of his smile left as he looked down at his clothing; she could sense he didn't feel comfortable with the idea of being at the dance. She wondered if he didn't want to embarrass her or himself. She thought for a moment before she added, "Tanner. I want you to know I don't give a damn about what you are wearing."

Tanner was shocked; he sat up straight and stammered, "Mary… you swore?!"

Mary chuckled, "Yes. The cussing message made what I said very clear. Don't put me on a pedestal. That keeps you at arm's length. I've already learned enough about you that I admire. I can tell by your smile that you enjoy my company. So, are you coming to the dance?"

"Mary Jane Tremble, you are a mind reader."

Mary Jane smiled; she sensed he liked to even say her name, "I promise not to cuss again, as long as you keep me off that pedestal."

Tanner stood. "I have to go back to work."

Tanner stopped at the doorway and then added, "Mary Jane Tremble, it seems that every time I see you, the pedestal gets a little higher."

Mary Jane smiled at the compliment; her regard for Tanner also grew a bit more. She added, "OK! As long as you make it to the dance Saturday night."

Tanner smiled, he nodded and went back into the blacksmith shop to work.

Mary Jane hurried up the street and met her mom coming out of the mercantile. Her mom said, "You were right about the good looks. And a street urchin is a good description."

Mary Jane nodded, "I think he's a bit amazing."

Mary Jane's mom asked, "You said the judge threw him out of Kearney for fighting?"

Mary Jane nodded, "Tanner punched the judge's son no less, right in the nose. He was teasing Tanner because of his clothing. He wouldn't leave him be. Finally, he ripped Tanner's shirt. Tanner said he popped him in the nose and that was the end of it. He said it wasn't much of a fight.

"The kid must have told his dad. The dad had Tanner put in jail for the weekend, and then on Monday he was brought into court in handcuffs. The judge ordered him to stay in handcuffs until he boarded the train."

Her mom asked, "So, you don't see any meanness in the lad?"

"None. Even after that and everything he's gone through, he jokes about it. He's been here since Monday; he's working with Goran Burkhart."

Her mom was surprised. "He's working with Goran?"

Mary Jane smiled, "Yes. I took him there to sort of test his mettle. I'm surprised he got the job. Most people Goran turns away. He told Goran he would work for nothing so Goran could decide, so Tanner could prove himself. Then, Tanner said that after the first day, Goran paid him because he didn't have anything to eat. It sounds like he is doing well."

Mary's mom asked, "You said he ran away."

Mary Jane nodded, "He was an indentured servant in St. Louis; they were mean to him, then they sold him to a factory owner. He said the factory owner meant to keep them working at the factory beyond their indenture. Tanner said he only had a part of a year left, actually a few months left on his indenture; he decided to run away.

"Tanner ended up in Kearney, far enough away so that the factory worker couldn't find him. Tanner said that he learned of a couple of others that ended up at the factory; one was killed by the machines."

Mary's mom shook her head. "I've heard so many stories about mistreated orphans…"

Mary Jane gave her mom a hug and said, "I was so lucky you picked me."

Her mom returned the hug and replied, "You're not setting your cap for him just because he's an orphan, are you?"

Mary Jane thought for a moment before responding, "No, Mom. So far I have a lot of respect for Tanner because of what he has gone through and who he has become. But I know there can be a lot of the past, a lot of animosity that may work against him. So far he's very calm, very nice… I even swore today to check his reaction."

Her mom asked, "You swore?"

Mary Jane explained about being put on a pedestal and expressing to him that she was just like him, no better than he. Mary Jane added, "When I explained why I swore, he smiled that easy smile of his. Then he said the pedestal got a bit higher."

Mary Jane's mom laughed and asked, "Do you think he'll come to the dance Saturday?"

"I think so, but I would like to sew some patches in his pants and sew his pocket back onto his shirt. Today I saw another burn hole from the hot metal."

For some time, there was silence, then Mary Jane took her mother's hand. "Mom, I'll tell you again, it was the greatest day ever when you took me off from that orphan train."

Mary's mom nodded, "It was indeed the best thing your dad and I ever did."

Goran Burkhart looked out the front window and watched as Mary Jane Tremble sat down with Tanner; he noted she was responsible for striking up a conversation. He moved closer so he could get an idea of what transpired between the two.

Mary Jane had sent Tanner to him earlier in the week; the boy offered to work for nothing. Goran figured the boy sincerely wanted a chance to prove himself. When Tanner worked right through lunch the first full day, Goran reminded him to eat. The boy nodded and continued to work. Finally, Goran told him that he needed to eat or he would get sick; Tanner nodded again. After some probing, the lad indicated that he had no money; he had nothing to eat.

Goran recalled his own embarrassment; he recalled feeding the lad and paying him after the first full day. Tanner was working full days plus extra time each day. When he was into a given task, Tanner liked to see the job through. Goran figured the lad was special, and he already knew Mary Jane was an astute young lady who he saw helping troubled kids now and then.

After listening to Mary Jane, hearing her cuss, then hearing her explain her reasons, his appreciation of Mary Jane grew. Goran walked away thinking that both young kids were special; he thought he would watch a bit to see what happened at the dance. He smiled at the prospect and determined it would happen if clothing was an issue.

That afternoon, an hour before time to quit for the day and before the mercantile closed for the day, Goran Burkhardt stopped Tanner in the middle of a task. He said, "Time to quit for the day."

Tanner was confused; he was ready to work till dark; he had nothing else to do. Tanner glanced outside; there was still plenty of the day left, and he was afraid he was getting fired. His voice shook as he questioned, "Sir?"

Goran motioned that Tanner should take a seat on the anvil and could sense some fear of the outcome. Goran Burkhart was a huge man that Tanner learned was a very fair person who never had occasion to threaten or raise his voice at him.

Tanner sat on the anvil as directed, and Goran spoke as he handed him a piece of paper, "I want you to go next door to the mercantile. This paper will allow you to get a couple pairs of pants, a couple shirts, a pair of shoes, and some other items. When you get done at the mercantile, come back here and eat with the family. By the way, where do you sleep at night?"

Sheepishly Tanner admitted, "The last few nights, I've been sleeping in the woodshed at the rail station."

Goran thought it was something like that, but in a woodshed? He couldn't imagine finding a comfortable way to sleep in a pile of wood.

Goran grinned, "Tonight, it's not too cold out; you can sleep on the porch. We'll get you a couple of blankets, so you sleep well. I have to protect my worker and make sure you are fresh in the morning. "

Goran smiled and added, "That way I can get more work out of you."

Tanner nodded and eagerly replied, "Yes, sir."

Goran made it clear, "I'm joking about working harder. You are doing fine right now. Now you better get to the mercantile before they close for the day."

Saturday, June 7, 1879. Blacksmith Shop

Goran noted that Tanner sat out front on the bench eating a bit, probably hoping that Mary Jane would show up.

Alaina had heard nothing new while in her room; the bartender's admonition to let things go for a few days was evidently being heeded. Since she heard nothing new, she took time to write out the details of her eavesdropping and send a copy of them to the New York World in case she was found out and killed.

It was Saturday noon when Arvid's buggy passed the blacksmith shop of Goran Burkhart. Alaina had Arvid stop when she noted Tanner sitting on the bench outside having a bite to eat. "Arvid. Stop here for a bit. I have to talk to that boy."

Alaina got out of the carriage and stepped to the boardwalk, Tanner Randolph!?"

"Yes, Ma'am." Tanner smiled as he asked, "Miss Alaina Christianson, I thought you were from Kearney?"

Alaina quickly related her story and added, "So Tanner, we've both been booted out of Kearney by Judge Odell Swinton. How are you liking Denver?"

Tanner explained, "So far Denver is the greatest. A gal showed me here to this shop, and I got a job with about the nicest man in the whole world."

Goran Burkhart had almost a full week working with the lad; he felt Tanner to be a smart, polite, and very hard worker. Now, as he adjusted the harness display while eavesdropping, he shook his head in wonder as he was described as 'the nicest man in the world.

Goran decided it was time to quit eavesdropping and went in to eat with his family. He decided he would have to ask about the two of them getting booted out of Kearney; it sounded like an interesting story.

Alaina smiled, “Tanner, I am happy you are working and feeling good about your job. Where do you stay at night?”

“At first I slept in the woodshed at the railroad station, but when Mr. Burkhart found out, he let me sleep on his porch. When I save up enough money, I’ll find a place to sleep.”

“I’m glad you feel good about what you are doing. Do you have any questions or problems?”

Tanner smiled and slowly nodded his head, “There is a dance tonight, and I’ve never danced.”

“Tanner. That is a good problem to have. Don’t let that hold you back. The gals will be glad to help you. Where is the dance held?”

Tanner pointed about three blocks up the street, “I guess it is a town hall, and sometimes they gather there for church on Sunday.”

Alaina rose. “I’ll be going. If I make it to the dance tonight, I’d like to dance with you. Just to show you how easy it is.”

Tanner nodded, “I’d like that.”

Alaina stood. “I’ll let you finish your lunch.”

Alaina stopped and added, “Tanner. You are doing a good job at working at who you want to become. I think I’ve told you before, you are a very nice young man.”

The pronouncement felt so good and so needed that he had trouble speaking. He nodded and issued a heartfelt weak, “Thank you, Ma’am.”

Tanner felt fairly like he was floating for the rest of the workday. It was like his big sister just gave him a big compliment.

When they had an hour to go, Goran came to him and brushed off the anvil and said, “Tanner. Have a seat here for a bit; we have to talk.”

This time Tanner sat down without fear. Goran grinned and asked, “Tanner, you’ve been grinning all afternoon; do you want to tell me why?”

Tanner realized that one of the things he needed to do was share his thoughts and feelings; it was something, an ability, which he was lacking. Tanner nodded, “Yes, sir. Miss Alaina told me I was on the right path, and she said I was a good person.”

Goran nodded, “You’ve been working here for nearly a week, and I’d say that I agree with Alaina. I know as a worker you follow direction well, you work hard, and I trust you; I don’t have to watch over you.

“I do have a question you don’t have to answer: How did you get to know Alaina?”

Tanner spoke of his short stay in Kearney, meeting Alaina and doing some odd jobs for her, the teasing because of his clothing, getting his shirt ripped, then ‘popping’ the judge’s son in the nose. He spoke about spending the weekend in jail, then being escorted to the train even after Alaina reported to the judge that his son was the instigator.

Goran asked, “Why did Alaina move to Denver?”

Tanner shrugged. “I don’t know exactly. I don’t think it was because she saw the judge’s son rip my shirt, but the judge wanted her out of town for something she saw or knew. I’ll have to ask her exactly why.”

Goran asked, “Where did you come from before you ended up in Kearney?”

Tanner looked at Goran, one who he had come to trust. He felt he could answer without fear. Tanner wondered where in the world to start. He decided to just go backwards from Kearney.

“I was indentured to a man in St. Louis. Before too long my time would be up; when I turn 18, I will be free. The man I was indentured to ran a wagon repair shop, and he made things for other factories.”

“How many boys did he have?”

“There were three of us.”

“All indentured?”

"Yes, sir. All of us were indentured. We lived in a small room off from the shop."

"Was he good to you? Did he pay you well?"

"He didn't pay us at all."

"Not at all?"

"Yes. They were supposed to make sure we got to school. Tom, the boss, said that our schooling was working with metal."

"How long were you there?"

"More than two years, closer to three or four."

Goran felt much disdain for the man that he did not know… He also felt that working for the man, time stood still for the three orphan indentures because there was no change, no celebration, and nothing to note the passing of time.

Tanner added, "Then I ran away."

Goran shook his head and chuckled, "I guess I'd run away too."

Tanner added to the unfairness, "I would have stayed until my indenture was over, but he was going to sell two of us to a factory owner. We heard them talking. The factory owner was told that we had less than six months to go on our indenture. The factory owner laughed and said it didn't matter; we'd be there a whole lot longer than that. I think he meant to keep us there almost like a jail."

Tanner added, "The one we were working for, Tom Brandt, he was going to get two hundred dollars apiece for us. I didn't like the idea of being forced to stay there forever; I ran away that night. I hopped on a train and ended up in Kearney."

Goran asked, "The other boy, did he run away also?"

"No. I told him I was going to get away. He didn't seem to care. He even told me that he was going to tell Brandt. As soon as he was fast asleep, I sneaked out that night."

Goran shook his head. "Were you in an orphanage before you worked with Tom Brandt in St. Louis?"

"No. I worked on a farm in Iowa until the owner broke his leg; then he sold me to Brandt. Before that I was in an orphanage for a few years. I think the people who adopted me when I was born got sick and died, so I was put back in the orphanage."

"Your parents?"

Tanner shrugged. "I don't know what happened to them. I was told when I was about ten that, when I was born, I had a twin, Isaiah. I guess Isaiah may have died; the Mr. in charge of me said the orphanage didn't have any record of what happened to him. I guess sometimes the babies were sold or the records disappeared with the babies."

Tanner laughed, "I don't know if I was sold or if he had to pay someone to take me."

Goran laughed at the self-deprecating joke, "I would suppose that's a pretty common joke in and about an orphanage."

Tanner nodded, "Yeah. I didn't dream up that joke, but I've used it a few times."

Goran smiled, "Tanner. You've suffered quite a few bruises in your life, but you have a great attitude and outlook. Keep grinning. This thing we call life is a great thing if we can face it with a grin."

For Tanner it was good to tell of his past; it seems to release some of the burden, although many questions remained.

Goran rose and asked, "Are you going to the dance tonight?"

Tanner nodded, "I'm a bit nervous, unsure, but I'm going to go. I think there will be people I know there to make it a little less scary."

Saturday June 7, 1879.
The dance

The people started to gather about seven o'clock; the fiddler would start about fifteen minutes later. Close to the entry there was a table for guns and a few hats. Another table was available for snacks that were typically brought by ladies for anyone to enjoy. Mary Jane Tremble put a box of cookies on the table and watched for Tanner to see if he would come. She thought if he didn't show up with his ragged clothing, he really couldn't be blamed.

The music started at 7:15 sharp; Mary Jane danced with her mother and father, and then she went to the table of snacks to see how her cookies were faring. She was greeted by Goran Burkhart. She looked up at the giant of a man; he smiled and asked, "Mary Jane. Would you do me the great honor of having this dance with me?"

The invitation was surprising to Mary Jane; she curtsied, smiled, and offered her hand, "I certainly would, Mr. Burkhart."

Mary Jane noted that Goran was a surprisingly good dancer. He stated, "I wanted to thank you for sending Tanner to me. He's a very good worker and a good person. Do you think he'll show up at the dance?"

"I hope so. But I wouldn't blame him if he didn't. His clothing was embarrassing to him. It would give him a legitimate reason for not coming."

As Goran towered over Mary Jane, he glanced at the door and watched as Tanner entered along with Alaina. Tanner was immediately given a dance lesson. Goran replied, "Mary Jane, I have a lot of faith in Tanner, and I wanted you to know that I have a lot of respect for you and what you stand for."

Mary Jane was surprised and a bit taken aback. "Thank you." She wondered what in the world Goran knew about her. Did her mom or dad talk to Goran about her?

Mary Jane decided to be upfront: "Mr. Burkhart, when I sent Tanner to you asking for a job, I had two things in mind. He needed a job, and I was testing him to learn more about him. To see if he had the backbone and strength of character needed to get that job, to even talk to someone as imposing as you, Mr. Burkhart.

"You see, Mr. Burkhart, someone with Tanner's background has to be able to stand tall, to fight to make it in order to succeed. In most cases they won't get any help. If one has been beaten, used, or abused all their life, it is hard to stand up. Sometimes it is easy to hide and take handouts or steal what is needed."

Goran didn't want to admit that he had done some eavesdropping; he noted, "You have a bit of insight. Tanner has arrived. I see he's getting some dance lessons from Alaina. Do you know Alaina?"

Mary Jane looked and replied, "No. I'll have to ask Tanner."

The dance was nearing the end; Goran stated, "Mary Jane. I've watched you help other newcomers to our fair city. At one time I thought you were a young busybody. I want you to know, Mary Jane, your insight and your charitable use of that insight to help others is a great gift that you use very well. I want you to know, in my book, you can do no wrong."

Mary Jane smiled, "That is very nice. Thank you."

Goran had an urge to tell her that he put her on a pedestal just like Tanner has.

Alaina showed up at the dance shortly before Tanner; as soon as he arrived, she took him onto the dance floor and started with dance lessons. It was a waltz; he caught on very quickly. After a bit, she told him to look up at her and not his feet. After a while she asked about his new clothes; Tanner spoke of Goran's advance so he could purchase them. She asked, "It seems like Goran is very good to you."

"Yes, ma'am. He's a very nice man. He's here now dancing with Mary Jane, the girl that took me to Mr. Burkhart's shop. Mary Jane is also a very nice gal."

Alaina smiled, "It sounds like you are doing well in Denver."

"Yes. I like Denver."

Alaina wanted to give him an out in case the world came tumbling down. "Tanner. If you ever get tossed out and don't know where to turn, come and see me. I have a bunch of people that I know can help. Before we leave tonight, I'll introduce you to my driver, Arvid. Arvid will know how to contact me. I know of a family that will take you in and treat you like a son. They will also give you great schooling opportunities. If you are troubled, if there is a problem too big to handle, get in touch with Arvid and come and see me."

"Yes, ma'am. Thank you. I… it is... it is good to be able to have someone to go to."

"I believe in you, Tanner."

Tanner's head nodded; he couldn't respond; someone believed in him. Someone validated him as a person. He was so emotionally drained he could but nod his thanks.

Alaina asked, "Would you like to dance with Mary Jane?"

Tanner nodded, "Yes. But she is dancing with Goran."

Alaina informed, "When at a dance such as this, you just tap the man on the shoulder and ask, 'May I have this dance? The polite thing for the gentleman to do is to bow and allow you to dance. In this case, you ask Goran if he would be so kind as to trade partners."

Tanner smiled, with Alaina guiding him. He was game; they moved beside Goran. Tanner tapped him on the shoulder and said, "Would you like to change partners?"

Goran smiled and bowed; Mary Jane smiled and curtsied.

As they danced, Goran smiled and admitted, "Alaina, I wanted to talk to you about Tanner. Was the partner exchange his idea or yours?"

"It was my idea. But it wasn't hard to convince Tanner of the exchange; I think Tanner is a bit smitten with Mary Jane."

Goran nodded, “Mary Jane is a great young lady, and Tanner talks very well of you. He mentioned your meeting in Kearney and getting booted out by the judge. I was wondering, why would the judge pick a fight with you?”

Alaina knew that the more she told Goran, the more he would understand her secret when the article came out in the New York World paper. Alaina also knew how important it was to have people she could rely on in a hurry. Given Tanner’s belief in him, Alaina thought Goran would be a valuable friend.

Alaina explained, “Goran. Tanner told me you are about the nicest man in the world. I will tell you about the Kearney judge as long as you promise not to retell the story.”

Goran didn’t understand why, but he agreed; Alaina told him the entire story. She summarized, “On two different occasions in one week, I saw the judge enter and leave the abode of one of the ladies of the night. It is a curious thing about some men in power; they think the position they are in gives them the privilege to run roughshod over someone they think is weaker.”

Goran shook his head. “If I ever get to Kearney, I’ll give the good judge a piece of my mind.”

“Thank you, Goran. Remember to say nothing; I will take good care of the judge.”

Goran now was convinced there was a lot more to Alaina than he thought previously. Goran grinned and asked, “I’m going to go have a dance with my wife, but before I go, did you know that Tanner could have had a twin at birth, and his name was Isaiah?”

“No. That is interesting. When I go back east, that will help.”

Tanner doesn’t know if the twin lived or died. The records were missing.”

The dance was over; Goran bowed and said, “If I can ever be of assistance, please let me know.”

“Thank you, Goran. In my line of endeavor, sometimes the help of a friend becomes necessary.”

Mary Jane’s thoughts of who Goran was grew while she danced with him, and now she wondered who Alaina was and her connection to the newly arrived Tanner. She was happy when Tanner took her in dance position. As they waltzed, she asked, "You learned to dance pretty fast."

"I'm not sure of myself yet, and Alaina said there are other kinds of dances to learn. She said I should listen to the rhythm of the music."

Tanner smiled, "Mary Jane. You said I was keeping you at arm's length. Whew. I'm a bit nervous this close."

Mary Jane giggled at his honesty, "We'll have to do this a lot until it gets easier."

Tanner slowly shook his head, feeling as though holding her would never get to be old. Mary Jane grinned and said, "Who is Alaina?"

Tanner explained a bit of the Kearney connection and the judge's eviction of both of them; then he said, "She said if I ever got into trouble, she would provide help. She told me I was a good person; can you imagine that?"

Mary Jane laughed, "Yes, I can. Now, can you tell me about your new clothes?"

Tanner explained how Goran advanced him money for clothes and even asked if he would attend the dance. Finally, Tanner explained how much he liked Denver because of Goran and Alaina. He looked into Mary Jane's eyes and said, "And especially you, Mary Jane Tremble. You led me to Goran's shop. I don't know why you did, but it was one of the nicest things that has ever happened to me."

Mary Jane smiled. Besides being good to look at, she didn't want to admit she was also finding out if he had the character needed to ask for the job. It was another test to see if he had any chinks in his armor. And now she was finding that the more she knew him, the more she liked him.

Tanner danced several dances with Mary Jane, and he discovered how mesmerizing it was to be close to her. He got to dance with Mary Jane's mom, Goran's wife, and Goran's six-year-old son.

He met Arvid and was assured once again that he could find refuge in Alaina if need be.

Sunday, June 8, 1879.
Goldstrike Saloon

It was getting late in the afternoon when the man referred to as Griz downed his sixth drink; he was drunk and getting ornerier by the minute. Bill, the bartender, only pretended to take their money; the sooner he got them both drunk enough, the sooner they would go sleep it off.

That was the way it usually happened; today it didn't seem to be working. Bill heard Griz say to his partner, "Louie. We didn't get paid enough."

Louie wasn't faring any better; the two had their heads together, but with their drinking, Bill was shocked when he heard Louie say, "Yeah. I think I should go talk to Mildred."

Griz growled something unintelligible, then Bill asked, "You two want another drink?"

Bill poured the drink, hoping they would drink it and get drunk enough to leave. He knew Mildred was going to raise holy hell, and he figured these two were worse than the threat of Eddie with a loose tongue.

Griz reached for the drink, chuckled, and said loud enough for the bartender to hear, "We timed that damn slide perfect." He laughed and added, "Hell, the timing was so good we should get paid triple."

Louie laughed loud enough that the two other customers looked to see what was so funny.

Griz and Louie clicked their glasses and dove into their drinks, celebrating their cruel joke. Griz added, "Yer right. That damn family has so much money; we should get a lot more."

Griz looked up the stairs and said, "Damn, Mildred's getting company. We don't want to disturb him."

Again, they both laughed. Louie got off the barstool and said, "I'm finishing this drink, then I'm going to hit the sack. Tomorrow I'll see Mildred about noon."

Griz slid off from his stool and finished his drink, then followed Louie out the door."

After they were gone, one of the other customers asked, "Bill, what was that all about?"

Bill wiped up the bar, held up his hands, and replied, "Dunno, Arnie. But I know they would have been better off in church today."

Arnie laughed, but Bill was worried about just how much Arnie had heard.

It was after closing time when Bill went up to Mildred's room. As he came up the stairway, Alaina rose from her bed and filled her hand with the five-shot Remington Rider.

The door to Mildred's room was unlocked; Alaina assumed it was the bartender, Bill. They spoke quietly; Alaina put the glass to the wall and readied her pen.

Mildred must have seen the look on Bill's face. She barked, "Now what the hell is going on?"

Bill replied, "Keep it down. Griz and Louie were in the bar talking way too loud. Maybe Arnie heard a bit of it."

"What did they talk about?"

"A lot. They weren't paid enough, they mentioned good timing on the landslide. Louie said he was going to come see you tomorrow about noon."

Mildred, in an angry voice, replied, "I told those guys they should get out of town."

"You should have demanded they leave town. Now what's going to happen?"

"If Louie comes up tomorrow, I'll tell him to lay low for a few weeks. We won't know if Eddie can get his hands on the mine title till at least the afternoon on Monday. Who knows how fast Eddie will be able to get the house office door unlocked? Without that title we'd be out of luck. We'll have to kill the kid and then control Eddie. If that happens, the judge will help with Eddie."

Bill asked, "Are you going to see the judge?"

Mildred laughed, "He's avoiding me like I have a bad disease. I'll only contact him if this deal falls apart. Then it will be time for us to get the hell out of town."

Alaina made a record of the conversation:

M-Now what the hell is going on?

B-keep voice down. Louie and Griz were in

M—What the hell did they say?

B- they weren't paid enough for the good timing on the landslide. Louie will see you at noon tomorrow.

M- told them to get out of town.

B- should have demanded they leave

M-Louie comes up… lay low for a few weeks… Without the title, we are out of luck. I won't know if Eddie can get his hands on the title before noon. Without the title we are out of luck.

M- We'll have to kill the kid and then control Eddie. If that happens, the judge will help with Eddie.

B- Are you going to see the judge?

M- Contact the judge if the deal falls apart.

Alaina quietly crawled into bed; the Remington was right beside her pillow. She said to herself, "Now the kid has to go?"

"Who is the kid who has to die?" She shook her head, trying to recall the information from Arvid about the banker and his wife. Why were they on their way to see their mine in a buggy? Who were Griz and Louie?

She shook her head. It would be impossible to get this information to New York and back in time to do any good. It sounds like things could happen the very next day.

Can she trust going to the sheriff? So far the only trust she has built up in Denver is with a driver, a blacksmith, and a boy. Her landlord appears to be part of a double murder. How much can the driver be trusted? So far Arvid has been stellar. After some better thoughts of a possible young love budding between Tanner and Mary Jane, sleep finally came.

Monday June 9, 1879. Denver

Alaina awoke to stare at the ceiling. Her mind was alive with the controversy of what she had gotten herself into. This time she felt the least insulated from the wrong she was trying to right. This situation was different; she knew she had to act fast.

Could she accomplish her task and keep her identity a secret? Could she live through this?

She rose, secured the Remington in a ready position, and dressed. She had to get help, and she had to contact the authorities. Throughout this she hoped to retain her anonymity and stay alive.

With her notes in her handbag close beside her Remington, she locked up and headed to the café. She smiled with great relief when she saw Arvid sitting at the counter. She sat beside him and quietly asked, "Arvid,. Do you have plenty of time in your schedule today?"

Arvid smiled and spoke quietly, "I do. I have all morning, as a matter of fact."

Alaina answered with obvious relief, "Thank goodness. Very good. Arvid, does Denver have a sheriff or a marshal?"

Arvid answered, "A sheriff, but the Marshall is housed here also."

"Do you trust the sheriff and the marshal? Are they without question honest?"

"Yes, ma'am. We like our sheriff."

"Arvid. How far away is the sheriff's office?"

"About a mile."

Alaina ordered breakfast, then slipped three dollars down the counter to Arvid. She asked, "Could you go to the sheriff's office and arrange a meeting with him away from the view of anyone? And, if the Marshall is around, include him in the meeting? Totally private. Away from anyone. Arvid I need that secrecy; it may mean whether I live or die."

Arvid asked, "Will you be safe while I'm gone?"

Alaina patted her purse, smiled, and nodded, "Yes, but I'm going to eat left-handed today. Hurry back."

Alaina added, "Arvid. If something happens to me, have the sheriff search my purse."

Alaina hoped the marshal would be there; if he wasn't, then Arvid would have to act as a witness.

Alaina ate slowly and then went out front to sit on the bench in the sun and wait. She didn't have long to wait; Arvid's horse was starting to lather when he returned."

She climbed into the buggy and asked, "Did you have any success?"

"The sheriff agreed and indicated that the Marshall may be available. We'll see when we get there."

The meeting spot chosen was a recently abandoned cabin in a small grove of trees. Two horses were visible out front; the scene was scary for a petite easterner.

Alaina looked to Arvid and said, "Would you introduce me?"

Just inside the door, the sheriff and the US Marshall waited with questioning looks. The sheriff quickly made introductions: "I am Sheriff Darren Wilkes; this is my friend, US Marshall Benton Hays. We refer to him much of the time as Ben. Now, I'm given to understand it may take both of us to save your life?"

Alaina smiled and replied, "Sheriff Wilkes, Marshall Hays, thanks for responding. Before we are done, I hope we can save at least one more life. Sheriff, do you know who is going to inherit the estate of the owner of the bank and a mine, the estate of those who were killed in a landslide some time ago?"

The sheriff nodded, "Yes, of course. Young Randolph Kristofferson is due to inherit."

Alaina turned to Arvid and said, "Arvid, would you please get Randolph Kristofferson and bring him here? Tell him he is under arrest if need be, whatever it takes. He very well could be at the bank. If he is at the bank, tell him to lock his father's office and leave orders that no one is allowed in that office."

Not fully understanding, Arvid looked to the sheriff, who smiled; the marshal dug in his pocket and handed Arvid a deputy's badge. "Tell him not to argue with you."

When Arvid left, Alaina said, "Thank you, Marshall."

The sheriff smiled, "Arvid has a lot of faith in you, ma'am, and we are going to grant you some latitude. Now, do you want to tell us what is going on here?"

Alaina took a breath and began while digging out her notes, "It was only a week ago that I met Arvid."

The sheriff nodded, "Arvid filled us in. He said you wanted to live in a place where you could see the good and the ugly. He said you chose the Goldstrike Saloon's boarding room."

"Yes, indeed. I got in a lot deeper than I wanted."

Alaina shared the notes and all the details down to the near shooting of the bartender, Bill. Then she added to the story, "Do you know the names, Griz and Louie?"

"We've had them in as boarders now and then."

Alaina explained the situation and backed it up with her notes on the conversations.

The sheriff looked at the Marshall and shook his head, "Where do we start?"

The Marshall grinned, "Ma'am. You come to town, and we must jail half the population."

The Marshall took Alaina's hand and shook it, "Ma'am. I hope you are safe now. I want you to know you stuck your neck out on purpose, and you are lucky you are still alive. Thank you."

The Marshall gave his assessment of how they should proceed. "First of all,. We will wait here for young Randolph. Then I will go and arrest the judge."

Alaina added, “Marshall, I don’t want to tell you your business, but if you could get your hands on the judge’s title to the mine, I’m sure he may have already changed it.”

The Marshall nodded, “You are right again. I’ll see if I can get my hands on the title. If it has been changed, it will add evidence to our case. Sheriff, I’d say Mildred and Bill would be next in line, then Griz and Louie, then Eddie. I figure Eddie is the least dangerous.”

The sheriff’s head was shaking; he stepped up and shook Alaina’s hand. “The marshal is right; you are an amazing lady. And the Marshall and I have to tell you this. We may need your testimony. We will try to use your written information against each of them so that they tell on each other, trying to shed the blame. They are all in danger of hanging. And Alaina, we appreciate your information. If all the people had your willingness help make the world a better place, it would make our job very simple.”

The sheriff grinned, “If we can, we’ll keep you out of it; that way you can retain your identity. Arvid seemed to think you were writing a column now and then in the New York World under the name of Annie in Hiding.”

Alaina smiled, “Thank you so much. I want you to know this little trip to Denver has been a whirlwind of debauchery, but I’ve also met the absolute greatest people here also. Now, if Arvid’s keeping my secret, Arvid and I will have a lot to talk about.”

The Marshall got his horse and said, “Speak of the devil, here comes Arvid now.”

The sheriff added, “I see he has the lad with him. Let’s go out and explain all this to him and the boy.”

Arvid tied his horse while Randolph stepped out of the carriage. When Randolph turned to face them, Alaina said, “Tanner? What are you doing here?”

As Randolph Kristofferson approached, he said, “That is the third time this week someone has called me Tanner. Arvid called me Tanner.”

Alaina held her hand to her mouth; in shock, she approached Randolph. The sheriff asked, "Are you all right, Alaina? You are as white as a ghost."

Alaina fanned her cheek; to steady herself, she held on to the sheriff's arm as she stepped closer to Randolph. She said, "Isaiah Randolph."

The sheriff was just as confused as the lad; Arvid stood and grinned, and Alaina looked to Arvid. Arvid grinned and shook his head, "I didn't tell him a thing, Alaina; I'll let you do the honors in case there is a tear or two shed. I had a hard time talking all the way here."

Alaina took Randolph by the shoulders and said, "You have a twin brother right here in Denver by the name of Tanner. Tanner Randolph. When you were born, you were named Isaiah Randolph."

Emotionally shaken and near tears, she shook her head. "My goodness, Isaiah. Your brother Tanner is working with and staying with Goran Burkhart, the blacksmith. Arvid and I are going to take you there until it is safe for you to return to your home."

The sheriff got into the saddle, looked to Arvid, and said, "Arvid. You still have that deputy badge. Since Randolph here is going to lose his court-appointed guardian and the judge is out of the picture, I am giving you the job of finding a new guardian. This time do a better job than the judge."

The sheriff added, "And, Alaina and Arvid, fill the boy in on all the shenanigans, including the loss of his mom and dad."

The sheriff looked to the boy, "Randolph, or Isaiah, you will soon receive a lot of news. A lot of changes in your life will be fed to you during the short trip to meet your brother. A lot to take in, from pain to sheer joy, but I'll tell you this: the two people with you, there are none finer. Lean on them for whatever support or advice you need.

"As soon as we get done with a lot of arresting, we'll stop by Garon's place and let you know all is safe."

Annie in Hiding Part II

Brothers meet.

Monday, June 9, 1879

Arvid helped Alaina into the buggy and then directed, "Isaiah or Randolph, sit beside Alaina; she has a lot to talk to you about." He asked Alaina as he got in and sat beside her, "Are we going to see Tanner?"

Randolph Kristofferson, now Isaiah Randolph, was clearly most anxious to see his brother. Alaina smiled, took his hand and replied, "Yes, we'll be there shortly. It is incredible how much you two look alike."

Alaina quickly outlined what she learned about the death of his mother and father at the hands of Griz and Louie, the machinations of the judge to gain control of the mine, the owner of the Goldstrike, Mildred, and finally his uncle Eddie.

Isiah shook his head and said, "Even Uncle Eddie. Eddie couldn't have done the planning; Eddie just isn't that smart. He is most interested in where his next drink is coming from."

Alaina indicated that Eddie had convinced Isaiah's mother and father to go to the mine. Then Eddie's job was to go through the files and find the title to the mine so that the judge could change the title to his benefit."

Isiah shook his head. "The title to the mine is in the safe at the bank."

Isaiah shook his head at how stupid it was to rely on Eddie for any part of the plan. He wanted to know what interested him the most, “Tell me about my brother Tanner. How long has he been in Denver, and how did he get here?”

Alaina spoke of the short time she knew Tanner, the fight in Kearney, being jailed, then sent to Denver. She told of him getting a job at Goran Burkhart’s blacksmith shop, a bit about Mary Jane Tremble’s help, and a little about Tanner’s life before Kearney.

Isaiah shook his head. “I’ve been protected from all of that. I guess I drew the right straw. What in the world is an indenture?”

Alaina explained as they arrived at the blacksmith shop, Isaiah replied, "It sounds a bit like slavery to me.”

Alaina could do nothing but nod in agreement. “Isaiah, do you want me to introduce you to Tanner?”

For some time, Isaiah said nothing, then he shook his head. He smiled and asked, “I think I’m going to do this by myself. But would you be ready to pick up the pieces?”

Alaina nodded, “Isaiah. In spite of all he has been through, you have a great brother. I, Arvid, and Goran Burkhart will be close by to pick up any pieces, but you just take your time. I’ll be right outside the door.”

Arvid asked Goran, “Where is Tanner?”

Goran replied, “In the back working. Do you want to see him?”

Arvid waved Isiah forward; when Goran saw him, his voice was but a whisper, “Isiah?”

Isiah nodded; the big man was visibly moved. Goran replied, “Oh my God!”

Alaina instructed, “Isiah said he wants to try to handle this by himself.”

Goran patted him on the back and directed, “Right through that door; he’s making braces for wagons right now.”

Isiah made his way to the back room; Tanner was working with flat strips of iron, bending them. Isiah walked over and sat on a bench facing Tanner.

Tanner glanced up, first of all catching movement out of the corner of his eye, and then he looked again as the very mirror image of himself stared back at him with a sheepish grin. In disbelief, Tanner looked him over more carefully; his hair, eyes, face, height, weight—everything about him was like he was looking in the mirror. Finally, with a lot of hope in his choking voice, he asked, "Isiah?"

Isiah could not speak; he nodded his head, and Tanner went to him and held him while unabashedly crying. Tanner sat on the bench and wiped his eyes; he apologized, "I can't recall the last time I cried. I think I was at the orphanage."

Isiah wiped his eyes; Tanner added, "Isaiah, I didn't know if you lived or died. It always seemed to me that you were alive someplace. There were no records. One of the men at the orphanage told me I had a twin, and his name was Isiah."

Isiah asked, "Where were we born?"

Tanner shrugged. "Don't know for sure. The orphanage I was in, was in a town on this side of Chicago."

Isiah asked, "Did you ever think about going back to look?"

Tanner shrugged, "I wouldn't have a clue as to where to start looking, and ever since the orphanage, someone else has told me where I was going. What about you? What happened to you?"

Isiah shook his head. "I was adopted. My mother and father moved here to Denver to start a bank. A few years ago, he bought a mine that the owner wanted to get rid of. Father no more than bought the mine, and the gold vein opened up. Father has always had money; the mine made him very wealthy."

Tanner laughed, "I got an advance on my pay so that I could buy clothes; I'm in debt."

Isiah shook his head. "Not anymore."

Tanner shook his head. "Your mom and dad have room for a brother in the house?"

Isiah told of the entire scheme to steal the mine from his father by the judge, then added, "I am left with a big house, a bank, and a mine. I have a cook who is like a big brother and a lady who takes good care of the house and a foreman at the mine. As soon as the sheriff arrests a bunch of people, we can go home."

Tanner shook his head; it was like a dream. "Home? Are you sure?"

"I'm very sure."

Again, Tanner was ready to break into tears. "Isiah, I've never had a home that I can remember, and big brother."

Isiah nodded, "Our home. You will like Art. And you're not getting too far out of my sight until I get to know all about you. We have a lot of catching up to do."

Tanner figured there wasn't much to learn about his past, other than work, "Outside of blacksmithing and farming, there isn't much to learn about me. I can't even tell you a good fishing story. I've never gotten the opportunity to go fishing."

Isiah laughed, "Art and I were going to go fishing tomorrow. Art is a great fisherman. He's mainly the cook, but he's also a member of the family, a big brother, a good teacher, and a great friend."

They talked for an hour before they decided to go out and talk to Alaina, Goran, and Arvid. When they appeared, Arvid smiled and asked, "You two didn't change clothes, did you? Do we still know Tanner from Isiah?"

Isiah answered, "We didn't change clothes. Alaina, thank you for all you do. Arvid, having someone that one can trust is the greatest thing in the world. Goran, from what Tanner has told me, you are the greatest person in the world, and since you took a chance on him, I want you to know that our family debt to you goes way beyond your advance for clothing. As Tanner explained, your kindness, your empathy, your acceptance, and your smile made him feel more alive and part of this world than ever before in his life. At birth we were somehow separated. I was very lucky; Tanner wasn't so lucky, but people like you three finally made him feel good. We thank you."

Arvid responded, "Thank you, Isiah, for including me. The sheriff gave me the responsibility to appoint someone to look over you and your estate until you turn eighteen. Either one of these two would be happy to take on the job. We decided that Alaina would be a bit less encumbered by jobs and family. Alaina has indicated that she would see herself as one answering questions and guiding you two rather than making decisions. So, until the sheriff arrives with the; all clear for you to return home, you can stay here at Goran's."

Alaina asked, "How does that sound with you boys?"

Tanner shrugged, and Isiah smiled, "Alaina, the bank pretty much runs itself, and so does the mine. Tanner and I are going to spend a lot of time together. As I indicated to Tanner, our cook is like a member of the family, and he is also a great teacher and fisherman. All the important things in life. When we need advice, Tanner has indicated that you are very trusted. As I said, because of you three, we both feel very lucky."

It was almost time to think about getting something to eat when the marshal and the sheriff showed up. The sheriff spoke, "We rounded up the entire bunch. I got some help from four deputies. The Marshall can tell you about the judge. Eddy will probably wake up in jail."

The Marshall chuckled as he explained, "When I got to the judge's office, I took your advice, Alaina. I told him that the mine ownership was in question, and I didn't know about the bank. The judge dug the title out of his desk and showed it to me. According to the judge's title, the judge is the owner of 95 percent of the mine. When we find the original, we'll know that along with murder, we will know how much of a thief the judge is. I put the title in my pocket. Of course, the judge wanted the title back, but I told him the title was now evidence in his trial and that he was under arrest. After I handcuffed him, I explained all the arrests being made, and the charge was murder. The judge was a little bit angry."

The sheriff added, "The Goldstrike Saloon is now closed. We picked up Eddie and Griz sitting at the bar; Mildred was a little busy with Louie. The bartender, Bill, pulled his shotgun out from under the bar. He won't need to be hung. The short of it is I think you are safe to return home. I stopped at the house; Art will be ready for you three, or four. I told him you'd be hungry, and I filled him in. Alaina, if there is any trouble, you can rely on Art."

Arvid shook Goran's hand and said, "Good luck with you and your wife adopting one of the orphans. After you talked about adopting, it caused me to think, I'm going to bring up the idea with my wife."

Alaina explained to Tanner and Isiah, "Goran was so moved by working with Tanner that he's considering adopting one of the orphan train children."

The sheriff and the Marshall left; Arvid announced, "Next stop, the Goldstrike Saloon, so we can pick up Alaina's luggage."

When they arrived at the Kristofferson home, Art met them at the doorway with a big grin. He asked, "Do you need any help with the luggage?"

Tanner looked at Isiah and said, "He's Black. I had a friend at the orphanage that was Black; he was funny, and he loved to laugh."

Isiah nodded, "That describes Art well. Art is a great cook, and he's one of the smartest men I know. The most important thing is he loves to go fishing."

Tanner held out his hand to Art, "Art. It is nice to meet you. I was just telling Isiah that a good friend in the orphanage was Black. When I was sent out on the orphan train, I lost track of him. He was a funny kid, and it seemed he had arms a mile long. Art, this is Alaina. Alaina is our boss and mom until we turn eighteen."

Art smiled at Tanner's enthusiasm, "My, you two look alike! I have dinner ready to put on the table. Tanner, you may want to fire me after you taste my cooking."

Tanner grinned and shrugged, "We're going fishing tomorrow; Isiah said you were a great fisherman, so the cooking won't matter quite as much. I've never been fishing, and Isiah said you were a great cook."

Art seemed to appreciate Tanner's open honesty, "Well then Tanner, we'll get an early breakfast, and we'll get to the fishing hole when they are biting. Are you an early riser?"

Tanner shrugged, "In the orphanage if we didn't get out of bed in a timely manner, we'd get a cold glass of water in the kisser. I wake up and get moving easily."

Art grinned, "When I wake you up in the morning, I'll bring along a pail of cold water just in case."

Isiah loved the banter between the two of them and the obvious acceptance of Tanner of the cook. Art took one of Alaina's bags and led them to the dining room where they had a sumptuous meal.

They decided to leave early for fishing; Alaina would stay behind; Alaina had some writing she wanted to do.

The fishing hole
Tuesday June 10, 1879.

On the stream there was a deep undercut bank, the lair of some pretty good-sized trout. After a while, Tanner asked, “How did you make your way to Denver Art?”

“I met Randolph Kristofferson on the train; I was a porter. He couldn’t sleep very well, so we talked for much of the night. He invited me to join him and his family. I liked him. He had just adopted Isiah; he said I was an intelligent man, and he enjoyed talking to me. I was staying in St. Louis; there were a lot of people in St. Louis that didn’t like me because of the color of my skin. My color didn’t matter to Randolph; he was more interested in me as a talented man. So, I tagged along as chief, cook, bottle washer, teacher, diaper changer, and fishing guide.”

Tanner nodded, “Mighty lucky for Isiah.”

Art asked, “Why do you say that?”

Tanner, while busy trying to entice a trout, responded, “Now that Isiah’s mom and dad are gone, you are all the family he has left.”

Art grinned and asked, “Family?”

Tanner nodded, “Yeah. Isiah said you were part of the family. Art, didn’t you ever have the desire to meet some gal, get married, and have a bunch of kids?”

Art slowly shook his head. “A long time ago I was married to that railroad station as a porter. I’ve never had the desire to find a mate and have kids. Like you said, I have always felt like I was a part of the family right here. I’m happy. Now, I feel like I have another little brother.”

"Besides being a big brother, Isiah said you were his teacher; he didn't tell me you were from St. Louis. I was indentured to a man from St. Louis."

For the next hour they spoke of Tanner's indenture and his sale to the owner of a factory that intended to enslave him way beyond his eighteenth birthday, which would be the legal end to his indenture.

With similarities mentioned, Art asked, "Roland Greenlee?"

Tanner nodded, "Yes. How did you know?"

"That man hired some of my friends; they had to run away from him too. They said he was the meanest man they ever met. Paid them just enough to keep from starving. I always wanted to go back and whup the tar out of that man."

Tanner looked at Isiah, who was busy hauling in a trout. "What do you think, Isiah? Let's talk to Alaina; I bet she could tell us how to cook that guy's goose. If Art whups the tar out of him, Art could end up in jail."

Isiah landed his trout in time for one to bite on Tanner's line; in less than two hours, they had plenty of fish. Isiah responded as he put his trout on a stringer, "I think you are right. Alaina knew what she was doing with my uncle Eddie, the judge, and his cronies. I think if we dig up the evidence and the people that were hurt, Alaina can find her way to get the punishment taken care of by the authorities, so Art doesn't have to whip the tar out of him."

Isiah looked to Tanner and Art, "When we get done in St. Louis, we can maybe head east and see if we can dig up where we were born and maybe even find out about our parents."

Tanner pulled his trout out onto the bank; he slipped it on the stringer and asked, "Should we wait till we are eighteen?"

Isiah smiled, "We don't have too long to wait, and we have some things to do here in Denver before we go. I have to find the original title to the mine, and since Eddie isn't around to dig in the files, I'll have to do some searching. Maybe Dad has put information about where we came from into a file. Then again, we must be prepared in case we never do find out about our origin."

With a smile, Tanner held up his hands. "I feel mighty good. I now have a family, a twin brother, and a big brother that knows how to fish." Then Tanner added, "And he's a mighty good cook."

Art indicated that they would drop off Isiah at the bank so he could continue his search through his father's files for the title to the mine. Art asked, "Tanner, do you want to help your brother?"

"After I get done learning how to clean the fish, I'll come over to the bank."

Art laughed, "You have your priorities straight."

While eating trout that evening, Alaina laughed at how excited Tanner was about learning how to fish and then how to clean the fish. She asked, "Tanner, are you going to learn how to prepare the fish next?"

Tanner was adamant; there was no way that Art could be replaced as cook, but he would enjoy watching. Alaina then stated, "Isiah has found the title to the mine and has shared the original title with the Marshall. It seems that the good judge has turned the percentages around. The judge owns only five percent, and due to some improvements both sides agreed upon, the good judge owes a bit of money to you boys."

Alaina asked, "What else did you accomplish, Isiah?"

Isiah smiled; he looked at Tanner as he answered, "I paid one of our family's bills."

Alaina asked, "Family bills?"

Isiah smiled and nodded. "Tanner owed Goran seven dollars. Our bank wrote Goran a check for twenty dollars; Francis took the check to Goran along with the papers indicating that our bank bought Goran's loan on his business. The going rate for his loan was eight percent. Goran is now paying one percent."

Alaina was astounded. "That was a very kind and thoughtful thing to do, Isiah. Tell us about how much that will save Goran per month for our interest."

Isiah proudly smiled, "Over twenty dollars a month. I had Francis tell Goran that if he does adopt, or if any questions arise, the bank will renegotiate. Francis told me that Goran was a very happy man. We are going to have to stay in contact with Goran and his family."

Isiah looked to Art, then Tanner. "Did you get an opportunity to talk to Alaina about St. Louis?"

Tanner was all smiles as he explained, "Art wants to go to St. Louis to whale the tar out of Roland Greenlee. Greenlee's the owner of the factory that purchased my indenture from Tom Brandt. Isiah and Art said that you could help us with Roland without Art having to go to jail for beating the guy up."

Alaina smiled and explained, "I think going to St. Louis is a good idea. I've had some dealings there; I think I can keep us protected while we gather the evidence. We'll need the names of the other boys that Tom Brandt had working for him. They will no doubt give us other names. Brandt can be prosecuted for buying kids and selling them. The same is true of Roland Greenlee. I think, if he is responsible for keeping people working against their wishes, that will come with a hefty fine and money for restitution."

Tanner asked, "What is restitution?"

Alaina explained, "Restitution is paying back the people that were hurt, stolen from, or harmed."

Alaina hesitated then added, "Tanner, the farmer that sold you as an indentured servant, can also be prosecuted. The people that put you on that Orphan Train, I don't think they ever came back to check up on you. That has to be addressed also."

Art was shaking his head. Finally, he smiled and said, "I told you boys that she would know what to do. Now, I'd like to go back there even more. I know I can find some people that got burned by that louse, Greenlee."

Isiah asked, "Two questions. Tanner and I do not have much time to go until we reach eighteen. Should we do this now, or should we wait till we turn eighteen? The next question would be, after we get done in St. Louis, should we go looking for our mother and father to see what happened with them?"

Alaina shrugged. "First of all, the trout was delicious. The best ever. As to your age, I don't think it will matter. We can go to St. Louis when you are ready. But you haven't exhausted all the places here that may give you knowledge of your birth parents. Tomorrow I'll help by looking through the files here in the office. You and Tanner go to the bank, or Tanner can help me here.

"I also have another suggestion that you can think about; that is, you may want to introduce your brother Tanner to your friends in the Denver area."

Tanner nodded, "I know how to dance now. Have you ever had a dance here in your main hall?"

Isiah shrugged. "We've had a lot of get-togethers; we've had musicians play for us; I guess we've never had a dance. I'm game to give it a go. Sounds like fun."

Alaina added, "The dance would be a good idea. I think I must check with the Marshall to see if he needs me here as a witness. If not, after the dance we could make plans for going to St. Louis; afterwards, we'll see. There is no need at this time to hurry."

The saloon in Kearney, Nebraska Wednesday June 11, 1879

J.B. Carmine wondered why he received twenty copies of the New York World newspaper, there were only five residents of the budding town of Kearney that subscribed. It was a little past noon, he usually read his copy later that night after returning home. J.B. Spread his copy on the bar, he wanted to know why he was sent so many copies. One of the columns on the front page in large print, read:

Kearney, NE. Kangaroo Court
Judge Odell Swinton Presiding.
Reporter, Annie in Hiding.

J.B. Carmine wasn't a fan of the judge; he smiled as he read:

On Friday, May 29, 1879, an orphan lad new to Kearney was accosted by the judge's son, no less. After much taunting and berating and getting no response, the judge's son ripped the pocket nearly off the shirt of the orphan lad. Whereupon the orphan lad 'popped' the judge's son in the nose.

The judge's son went home and complained to his father. With no investigation as to fault, the good judge told the sheriff to lock up the orphaned lad for the entire weekend.

The following Monday, June 2, acting under the judge's orders, in the words of the sheriff and the bailiff, the very compliant and polite orphan lad was led in handcuffs to the courtroom. The only business of the day, court convened at 11 AM; within fifteen minutes the lad was sent out of town on the noon railroad bound for Denver.

The trial in the mind of Annie in Hiding was a travesty of justice, but the real story begins.

After being informed who the witness to the altercation was, one undercover lady, Annie in Hiding, no less, just happened to observe Judge Odell Swinton on two occasions within the week, once coming and once leaving the accommodations of one who shall go unnamed, who the townspeople refer to as, "The lady of the night," and, "What's her Name."

The good judge, with no evidence, no meeting, decided that Annie in Hiding was "indigent," and she was summarily escorted out of town.

Annie in Hiding says, "Upon boarding the train, I made a promise to the good judge that I would write. So, here it is, Mr. Odell Swinton.

During my short time in Kearney, I've been told that from the bench you've used a rather comical form of humiliation as punishment called being tarred, feathered, tied to a rail, and removed from town. My usual recommendation is a good horsewhipping, but I'll leave your punishment up to the good people of Kearney. I wish you all a bit of humor in dealing with the good judge."

With no customers in the saloon, J.B. Carmine took the papers and rushed out the door with a smile. There was a tradition that started in Kearney, a late afternoon gathering at Gertie's Café. J.B. wanted everybody to read the paper and meet at Gerties. Everybody had to be informed, except the judge; to the judge, the gathering would be a surprise.

Judge Odell Swinton arrived at Gertie's a little before five o'clock. There were already a few people there who seemed to ignore him; he took a seat at the counter and asked for a cup of coffee. Gertie poured his coffee and turned away; the judge thought she was close to laughter. The café filled rapidly; it seemed to the judge there were more people, smiles, and laughter than usual. At five o'clock the bailiff entered with a gallon pail of tar and sat it in the middle of the floor.

As if on cue, everyone quieted. Jim Swenson loudly asked the obvious question, "What do you have there, Mr. Thompson?"

The bailiff smiled and loudly reported, "Why, that's a bucket of tar, Jim."

Next to arrive was Sadie Smith, a seamstress, who put a bag down next to the bucket of tar. As everyone quieted, Jim loudly asked, "What do you have there, Sadie?"

The entire place was quiet now. Sadie answered, "Why, that's a bag of feathers, Jim."

Right behind Sadie, Tom Brown came through the door with an eight-foot-long pole; everyone quieted as he laid the pole on the floor beside the tar and feathers. Jim asked, "What do you have there, Tom?"

With everyone's eyes on Tom Brown, including the judge, Tom looked down at the pole and gave his pre-scripted answer. "Well, that's a rail, Jim. We'll need that for the tar and feathers."

At the same time, on cue, a few snickers were heard as J.B. Carmine entered and sat down beside the intentionally vacant seat next to the judge. He slid the judge's copy of the paper in front of Judge Odell Swinton. Now the place was very crowded; most were chuckling. J.B. advised, "Maybe you should read the front page article about Kearney."

There was quite a bit of laughter as quiet stories were shared amongst the crowd. When the judge completed reading the article, he sat frozen; he was the brunt of all the humor, and the tar and feathers were a direct result of Annie in Hiding; the tar and the feathers were meant for him.

J.B. Carmine advised, "I think if I were you, I'd bolt out through the kitchen and then get out of town as quick as I could."

The judge's head lowered as though he was thinking about how best to take J.B.'s advice. Suddenly he bolted out through the kitchen and didn't stop running till he got home. All the way he was thinking about ways that he could get back at Annie in

Hiding. He didn't give much thought to whether his wife or son read the paper.

That same day, an hour before the five o'clock get-together at Gertie's Café, a copy of the paper was given to Caroline Swinton, wife of Odell Swinton. She quietly packed her bags; there was a train scheduled to go east at five o'clock, the same time the judge would be meeting at Gertie's. His philandering was the 'final straw.'

She circled the article, and above it she wrote, "Goodbye." She left the paper on the desk at the front of the house; she figured her son hadn't yet learned what humility was; the two of them deserved each other.

As the judge approached his house, he could hear the chugging of the train as it left the station heading east. His next best getaway would be the noon train to Denver the next day. Not knowing exactly whether the townspeople planned to follow through on the tar and feathering, he felt he had to lay low. Finally, he asked himself, 'What will my wife think?'

Upon reading the "Goodbye" written on the newspaper article, he figured he wouldn't have to worry about his wife or his son; they were gone. He checked their safe; most of the money was gone, he had a bit hidden in his dresser. He packed a bag so that he could be ready to walk away, and he slipped a small two-barreled Derringer into his pocket.

He figured he would hide until noon the next day; he remained dressed as he lay on his bed. An hour into his wait, the front door shut, and footsteps were heard coming his way. He got up and quietly opened the door with the Derringer in his hand. There wasn't much light in the house; he leveled the gun at the image coming his way. When he was about to pull the trigger, he recognized his son.

The judge snapped, "Wilbur! I damn near shot you. I thought you left town with your mother."

"Where did she go?"

"I think to her sister's, your Aunt Ester's. She's been talking about going to her place for three years now."

Wilbur laughed, "Hell, I didn't get an invitation. She's been telling me for a couple of years now that the two of us deserve each other. Dang, they kept that tar and feather business a big secret. She somehow must have read the paper."

"Yes. Did you?"

"Hell yes. I told you this was too small of a town to be diddling that woman. They told me down at the saloon about the tar and feather threat; they said that you would be home packing your gear for travel. That Alaina woman you told me about, she nailed your kiester pretty good, didn't she?"

The judge nodded, "Tomorrow I'm heading to Denver on the noon train; maybe I can bump into her if she is still there. Since she's a reporter, she could be on her way back home, wherever that is.

"Well son, I'm not sure what we are going to do there to make a living; your mother about emptied the safe."

Wilbur again laughed, "Since I didn't get an invitation to go with Mom, I'll tag along with you, who knows, and maybe I can bump into that orphan."

The judge nodded, "I've got enough money left to hire someone to help me do away with that woman."

The next day on the way to the train station, three times they heard people shout, "Get the tar and feathers."

They got their tickets and waited out of sight on benches outside the station waiting room. The judge quietly informed, "Wilbur. When we get to Denver, we'll have to lose our last name. That damn paper's story will be all over Denver and the rest of the country. We'll use a different last name; how about Smith?"

Wilbur laughed, "Wilbur Smith. Sure. How long are we going to be staying in Denver?"

Just long enough for me to waylay that woman. Then we are getting out of there in a hurry, probably heading east."

"If you go to Aunt Ester's, you are going to have to eat a lot of crow."

Odell scoffed, "I'm not about to bow or kiss her ring."

Wilbur laughed, but he knew if he decided to go to his Aunt Ester's, he would have to tow the mark; he'd have to do an awful lot of ring kissing.

The birth certificates. Denver, June 11, 1879

It was nearly noon; Isaiah had been looking through the files most of the morning when Tanner raced in. Tanner's voice showed his excitement, "Isaiah, come on home. Alaina found a file about our birth. It even has both of our birth certificates in it."

Isaiah closed and locked the door to the office and ran with Tanner the short distance to the house. Alaina met them in the living room at a small table; Art was there; he was all smiles. He related, "I think you boys will be a bit happy when you get done here."

Alaina explained, "I found your birth certificates and a letter from your dad, Isaiah. Can I read the letter from your dad first?"

Isaiah nodded; Elaina read:

Dear Isaiah Randolph,

Yes, your name at birth was Isaiah Randolph. I named you Randolph, my name, and I want you to know that having you as a son was the best decision your mom and I ever made.

The reason I waited till you turned eighteen to tell you about your birth parents… I guess I didn't want you running off to do your own investigating. I figure when I tell you, you'll be heading east to find your twin brother Tanner.

Yes, you have a twin… We made it to the hospital a day late, or I think Mom would have adopted both of you. Your brother Tanner was taken a day earlier. I asked for and received copies of both birth certificates. The birth certificates have the names of your parents and the city where you were born.

I decided to write this in case you demand to go searching for your birth family; that way you would have more information to go on. Also, just in case something happens to me where I am unable to relate this information.

The most important part, I repeat, you were the best decision your mom and I made in our entire lives.

Happy birthday, Son. Whatever you choose to do, you will have our support.

Love, Mom and Dad.

Isaiah had tears in his eyes; Tanner put a consoling arm on his shoulders, and Isaiah nodded and said, "It makes me think about how lucky I was. I wish they were still alive right now to see that Tanner made it back into the family."

Isaiah and Tanner looked over their birth certificates. Tanner exclaimed, "We were born in Westchester, Illinois, to Louise and Gunnar Randolph. They list their home as Kane County. The orphanage I was in was in Westchester."

Tanner grinned and then said, "I wonder if Mom and Dad ever tried to check up on us there. Actually, I suppose since I was taken away from the hospital, there would be no reason to look for us at an orphanage."

Isaiah nodded, "Louise and Gunnar Randolph. Louise, Gunnar… I wonder if they are still alive."

Tanner shrugged, "We'll just have to go see."

About that time there was a loud knock at the front door. Art started for the door, and Tanner stepped in front of him and said, "I'll get it, Art."

Art had a huge grin; he felt in the eyes of the boys that he was indeed treated like a brother, a part of the family. He watched in the hall as Tanner opened the door. Tanner exclaimed, "Arvid! You have good timing. Come on in; we just found our original birth certificates. We already mentioned going to see if our parents are still alive."

Arvid handed Tanner the paper and explained, "When I read this article, I knew you and Alaina would want to see it right away. I figured you'd be busy going through records. I can't stay; I have a customer waiting in the buggy. I would be interested in hearing Alaina's reaction to the article, though."

As Tanner handed the newspaper to Art, he grinned and said, "Arvid said he'd be interested in your reaction to the paper, Alaina."

Art read the article to them. Afterward, Alaina smiled, "Now, I'm afraid my cover may well disappear, especially if Odell Swinton gets sent out of town tarred and feathered; then he could end up in Denver. We may have to head east sooner than we thought.

Art asked, "Alaina, you no doubt have family back east."

Alaina nodded, "Yes, I do. My family supports what I am doing, but they want me to come home and be done with this undercover reporting. They don't like the danger. Why did you surmise I had family back east?"

Art grinned, "You have the confidence of one that has plenty of support. I just figured you came from a pretty solid background, and I think very good parents."

Alaina nodded, "If we go that far back east, I'll have to introduce you all. Now, what is our plan?"

Tanner rose, "I'm going to get Arvid. I think he meets the train every day. We'll let him know about Swinton; maybe Arvid will have an idea."

Art rose and grabbed a jacket. "I'm going with Tanner. I'm pretty good at catching or outthinking a polecat. Maybe Arvid and I can figure out a way to tan Swinton's hide if he does happen to come this way."

Alaina looked at a grinning Isaiah and asked, "What are you so happy about?"

"Those two will have a big day tomorrow. Tanner has invited Mary Jane Tremble to go fishing in the morning with Art; I've been invited also. Would you like to go fishing with us, Alaina?"

"I'll talk to Art first and see if he and Arvid have anything cooked up for Swinton; then I think I'll have to visit with the sheriff to see if I can leave town suddenly. I don't know if there is anyone in town other than the ones that are in jail and

Swinton that I have to fear. If my identity gets out, I'll have to leave in a hurry."

Revenge, failed
Thursday June 12, 1879

The train ride to Denver was torture for Odell Swinton; he stopped talking and became very sullen. Once in command, he now had to rebuild everything, including a way to earn an income. He had no wife, a son that was a liability, and the more he thought, the more hate for Alaina he developed.

Finally, his son spoke, "Dad. Christ. You are talking to yourself. Hell, I'd like to get back at that Tanner just as much as you want to hurt that Alaina, or Annie in Hiding, whatever she goes by, but you are going off the deep end."

"That woman ruined my life. I'd like to see her exposed; hell, I'd rather see her dead."

"Jesus! Don't talk like that."

"Why not? She ruined my life."

"You ruined your life by visiting 'What's her name". I told you it was a dumb thing to do in that little town."

"Who the hell's side are you on?"

"I'm on my side. I don't want to spend any time in jail. I'm talking about a poke in the kisser. You are talking about murder."

Odell's head lowered again. Meanwhile, Wilbur was now thinking that it may be necessary to do some ring kissing at his aunt Ester's home. He thought if he went to stay with his aunt Ester, then he wouldn't have to worry about spending time in jail.

It was a little after five o'clock when the train pulled into Denver; the station was crowded with the mix of people loading and getting off the train. The judge was all alone; his son was on his way back east, heading back to join his mother at his aunt's home.

The Denver station wasn't too busy. Odell wanted a place to stay and a way of gathering information. He went to the ticket counter and asked, "I'm from out of town; I'd like to find a place to stay and get information about Denver."

The man behind the counter nodded; the man fitted the description he was given. "You have a man right out front that can help you out. He knows Denver; he can help you with anything you'd like."

Odell muttered under his breath, 'Maybe he can help me take care of my problem.'

Arvid was waiting with his buggy; he already had a rider. Swinton questioned, "I'd like a ride to a boarding house and information on your fair city. The ticket salesman said you were the man to talk to."

Arvid grinned; the guy fit the description given him by Alaina and Art: "I'm your man. Hop in; I have to take this gent to the saloon to slake his thirst; a good place to stay isn't too far from there. Cost you four bits for the ride; the information is free."

On the way to the saloon, Swinton pumped the other rider for information but got little. He came all the way from St. Louis and left his bottle in the carriage on the way to the railroad station. For an Irish whiskey salesman, it was almost unheard of not to have at least a flask in his pocket. When the buggy stopped at the saloon, he jumped out and started toward the door before Swinton hailed him, "Hey, you left your bag in the buggy."

He came back, shaking his head. "I'm sorry. That's almost as bad as leaving my bottle in the buggy. I'm Angus Peet. I thank you. What's your name, my good man, and can I buy you a drink?"

"I'm Odell…" Damn, he didn't want to hand out his real name... "Smith. Odell Smith. Ahh, maybe later, I have to find a place to stay first."

As Angus disappeared in the saloon, Arvid asked, "Will you be staying long? I know of a spot a block from here operated by an old gal and her son. Two bits a night, five dollars a month."

Odell nodded. “That sounds acceptable. Will I have to share the bed?”

Arvid laughed, “If you want to share the bed, I know of another lady that owns a ‘house.’”

Odell grinned. Arvid was appealing to an interested side of him, but he didn’t want to seem too anxious. “First we’ll get me a room; maybe another time we’ll talk about sharing.”

Arvid laughed, “Anyone else I can get you connected with? Doctor, lawyer, beggar, thief?”

Odell chuckled, “I have a messy job to do; I don’t know. How handy is the beggar and thief?”

Arvid figured this was way too easy. “I tell you what. This is the boarding house. In the back of the boarding house is a shack; sometimes you can find a man out there whittling. You can’t miss him. I think for the right price you can talk him into just about anything. The guy also knows his way around Denver, and somehow he’s smart enough to stay out of jail.”

Odell asked, “What’s his name? I want to get the right person.”

“Art. You can’t miss him; he’s Black.”

Odell smiled; his color evidently appealed to his twisted sense of revenge. Odell handed Arvid the fifty cents and figured that he got a bargain. He expected to take days getting the information he got in one buggy ride. Hopefully he could get this job done and get out of town right away. The newly completed railroad went all the way to California. He heard the weather was quite warm in California.

When he checked in, he wanted it to look like he’d be around for a long time; he rented a room for a month. Once in his room, he made his way out the back door. He grinned as he saw a Black man leaning against the wall, sitting on a bench and whittling. The former judge, Odell Swinton, approached Art; he glanced about to make sure there were no prying ears.

Swinton asked, “Are you Art?”

Art looked up and nodded. Art was sure this was the man that Alaina and Tanner described, "Yass suh. I be Art. Now, firs of all, how'd ya'all git holdt of my name?"

"Driver by the name of Arvid."

"Okaaay… I like Arvid. I kin trust Arvid. What can I do fo ya'all?"

Swinton was blunt: "Arvid told me you may be able to carry out a rather nasty task in exchange for money."

Art smiled and nodded; he thought he would play with him a bit. "Yass suh. A nasty task?" Art brushed off the bench next to him and invited, "Sit yo sef down, yass suh, if the money am right, I'm yo man. How nasty a job is it? Do I have to run like hell when I gets done?"

Swinton continued to stand; he couldn't bring himself to sit down with a Black man. Swinton shrugged. "Yes. It may be advisable to get out of town in a hurry."

Art grinned at Swinton's inability to take a seat beside him. Art asked, "Do I gets to use my knife and do it quietly an sneaky-like, an I likes to mess em up a bit, do I git to mess him up a bit first?"

Swinton shrugged, "It's her, and you can mess her up all you want. The more, the better."

"My… What's your name suh?"

"Odell Smith."

"Mr. Smith, huh? So, you want her deaded?"

Swinton nodded. "Yes. I'd like her dead."

"Fifty dollars up front and fifty when the job is done."

Swinton offered another deal: "How about all of it, seventy-five up front?"

Art was laughing inside at how simple this was. Art offered, "Eighty up front, n' done."

Swinton again shrugged and began to dig in his wallet. "Eighty it is."

"Who is diss woman?"

"She came to town not too long ago; she goes by the name of Alaina Christianson, and Annie in hiding."

“Yass suh I knows da woman. It seems she’s not a mean sort, why you want her deaded?”

“That information I will keep to myself.”

Swinton didn’t want his relationship with her revealed; he wanted to protect himself.

Art shrugged, “No matters to me suh. When I do her in, you want I should tell her it was you that paid me to do it?”

He grinned and nodded. “Yeah, tell her Odell is getting revenge.”

“Yass suh. You hand over the cash, and I’ll do her in.”

Swinton counted out eighty dollars, whereupon Art hauled out a deputy sheriff’s badge and pinned it on and then spoke, dropping the slang. "Well, Mr. Odell Swinton, I’m afraid I’m going to have to place you under arrest.”

“Arrest! What for? I didn’t do anything!”

Art laughed as Arvid drove up in his buggy. “Since you were once a judge, I think you know the severity of what you attempted to do: hire a deputy to commit murder. For now, Arvid and I will deliver you to jail. You may have to stay in jail for some time awaiting trial; we just recently lost our judge. As a matter of fact, you’ll probably get to meet him in jail.”

Arvid stepped out of the buggy with a pair of handcuffs. After handcuffing Swinton, Arvid asked, “That was pretty fast. Was he adamant?”

Art smiled. “He even thought I should mess her up a bit and tell her afterwards it was Odell that was getting revenge. I think the judge has built up a lot of hate there.”

Arvid produced a pair of handcuffs; he put them on as he explained, “We’ll have to drop him off at the jail; the sheriff will want us to fill out a statement.”

Art got in and sat close next to Odell with a broad grin. Art asked, “Odell, are you going to behave yourself, or do I have to mess you up a bit?”

While Arvid burst out laughing, Odell wisely decided to remain silent.

Three hours later, Arvid and Art returned to the house to report to Alaina and the twins. After an hour of laughing at the expense of Odell Swinton, the door knocker was heard. Arvid rose and explained, "I'll get it. I have a feeling it's the sheriff."

Soon Arvid returned with the sheriff; they were both chuckling at the day's events. The sheriff asked, "I hear from Arvid that you are going to St. Louis to round up a few more judges."

Alaina laughed, "We are still looking for permission to leave town. We'd like to take Arvid with us, but I don't think his wife wants him gone that long."

Arvid nodded and replied, "And I better be getting home. It's been a long day."

Tanner spoke, "Arvid. You've helped to make us safer. There is no telling what may have happened if you wouldn't have gotten to Swinton first."

Alaina nodded. "Tanner is right. Thank you again, Arvid and Art. You've perhaps saved my life. Sheriff, is it alright if the boys and I head to St. Louis for a bit?"

"I don't have a judge for replacement coming in here for at least two months. Those two judges will have a lot to talk about at that time. Before you go, all I ask is that you keep in contact; send a letter or a telegraph with a way that I can contact you."

Alaina wrote down the name of her father and explained, "I try to make sure he knows where I am and what I am about. Please do not contact him unless necessary, and whatever you do, do not disclose his name to anyone."

The sheriff looked at the name and said, "I am impressed. I will contact him only if it becomes an absolute must. It has been a pleasure to know all of you. When do you plan on leaving town?"

Alaina explained, "Now that Swinton is behind bars, we have to worry about him talking. I think we will be going very soon."

The sheriff suggested, "Just go fishing or stay holed up for a couple of days. I'll keep the two judges apart and incommunicado for a couple of days. That will be just in case I need more information."

Part III
Retribution
The St. Louis Depot
Sunday, June 15, 1879

The train arrived at 9:30 at night; it was dark. Alaina suggested, "When I was here last, I stayed in a hotel just down the block, the Hotel St. Louis."

The foursome gathered on the sidewalk in front of the rail station. Art laid down the law. "Remember what we talked about while we were on the train. This city is a dangerous place for all of you. Make sure you stay together always."

Art put his hand on Tanner's shoulder and asked Tanner. "You said Brandt's place was close to the rail station. How close?"

Tanner stepped forward and pointed down the block to the west. It's that gray building that needs a paint job about two blocks from here.

Art admonished. "Stay away from there. Let the sheriff do any confronting. Don't be walking around the streets sightseeing. There are people that will recognize all three of you."

Art looked to Alaina. "Alaina. Where is Wilbert Stevens place from here?"

Elaina pointed to the east; it's about two or three blocks down past the hotel where we will be staying tonight. Don't worry; I'm not going to revisit his bawdy house. I think he's probably still in jail."

Art wasn't convinced. "Unless you hear that someone else is abusing those orphan kids, stay away from there."

Elaina smiled and said, "This time I'll let the sheriff take care of it."

Art was adamant. "You three stick together. Don't let anyone out of your sight."

Tanner laughed and replied, "Art, you told us to stick together about 10 times when we were on the train. We promise we'll stay together."

Alaina asked, "What are you going to do for the night, Art? The boys need you to be safe."

Art replied, "I'll be safe. I'm staying about three blocks from the hotel. I will meet with you guys in the morning at the café across from the hotel at eight o'clock."

It was a little before eight when they met in front of the café. Art asked, "What is on your schedule this morning?"

Alaina responded, "A little after nine this morning we will meet with the sheriff and talk about Tom Brandt. We will give him the names of the indentured kids that Tanner thinks Brandt sold to Greenlee, and then we'll let the sheriff direct us from there."

Art nodded, "OK. I'll be back here about noon. I'll be meeting with some of Greenlee's old workers and see what I can get out of them." As an afterthought, Art smiled and repeated, "Remember; stick together."

Tanner asked, "Are you eating breakfast with us?"

Art grinned and replied without elaborating, "I got a better offer."

Tanner asked, "Someone that cooks better than you do?"

Art just smiled. Alaina reminded, "Remember Art. The boys need you. Don't put yourself in any danger either. And don't look for a way to get revenge on the part of Tanner."

Art smiled and replied, "That's good advice. I'll admit I've had some of those thoughts."

After breakfast was completed, the threesome crossed the street; a half block to the west, they turned left and headed south toward the police station. The police station could be seen a few blocks away.

During the next block they were chatting about everything from joking about Tanner's girlfriend to fishing trout on the bank of the stream up in Denver with Art. When they came to the end of the block, Isaiah stopped short and exclaimed, Manny's!"

Tanner wondered, "Manny's? What is that?"

Isaiah explained. "Manfred Martin. He's the owner of the St. Louis National Bank right across the street from here. He is a very good friend of the family, and he's been a friend of Mom and Dad ever since they were kids growing up. I have to run over and say hello quick."

Alaina offered, "Perhaps on the way back. If we stop now, we'll be late for our meeting with the sheriff."

Isaiah shook his head; he was adamant, "You two go. I'll only be a minute; I'll probably be at the Sheriff's Office before the meeting starts. I can't go by Manny's without saying hello."

Tanner pleaded, "Are you sure it can't wait just another hour or so?"

Isaiah shook his head. "When Dad and Mom were killed, Manny and his family came to Denver a couple of days later and stayed with me for almost a week. Manny helped with all the funeral… I have to stop. I won't be but a minute. Later on today Tanner, I'll introduce you to Manny and his family. They are just super great people. Don't worry about me. You'll watch me go in the bank, and it is less than two blocks to the police station. For that distance I could outrun anybody."

Very reluctantly, Alaina and Tanner watched as Isaiah crossed the street and safely entered the bank. They then hurried on their way so that they would not be late meeting with the sheriff.

The sheriff met them at the door and took them directly to his office. Without Isaiah, Tanner was nervous; meanwhile, the sheriff had to rehash the arrest and conviction of Wilbert

Stevens and the others involved in the prostitution of the young orphan girls.

To Tanner it seemed forever before they got on the topic of Tom Brandt and the sales of indentured orphans to Roland Greenlee and the possibility that Greenlee was holding a few of them there against their will as actual slaves.

The sheriff asked Tanner, “And you specifically heard that Greenlee was going to keep you imprisoned to work.”

Tanner nodded, Yes, sir. Greenlee was paid two hundred for me. There were six others that I also gave the names to Art that may have been sold to Roland Greenlee.”

Tanner then added, “Sir, right now we’ve been here for almost two hours, and my brother Isaiah should have been here long ago. I feel that something is wrong. I’m going to the bank to check up on him.”

Alaina nodded. "I agree. We have to check up on him as soon as possible.”

Tanner shook his head. I sure hope Tom Brandt hasn’t seen him and mistook him for me.”

“You two look that much alike?”

“Yes, sir. It’s like looking in a mirror.”

As Isaiah crossed the street, he realized that he could be in danger, but he thought, certainly not at Manny’s bank. Upon entering the bank, he went directly to one of the tellers and asked, “Is Manny in?”

The teller asked, “Manny?”

Isaiah smiled at the use of the nickname, “Manfred Martin, the bank owner. Would you please tell him that Randolph Kristofferson is here and would like to say hello?

The teller went to another desk and relayed the information. Soon that person came over and spoke directly to Isaiah. “Mr. Martin is with his family this morning. He won’t be in until later this afternoon.”

Isaiah shrugged. “Would you tell him that Randolph Kristofferson was here and that I’ll drop by later this afternoon to say hello? Also, while I'm in town I'm staying at the St. Louis Hotel."

Isaiah walked out of the bank and turned the corner heading to the Sheriff's Office when he was suddenly grabbed from both sides by two men; each one took an arm. They practically carried him, and with a few cuss words, he was almost dragged into the alley. As they were rushing down the alley, Isaiah was slapped hard behind the head.

The one on his right spat, "I don't know what the hell you were doing in that bank, but now your fanny is mine."

Isaiah knew the one that hit him was Tom Brandt. Based on lessons learned from Tanner, he knew to say little and expect to be treated as though his life didn't matter.

Brandt laughed derisively as they turned the corner and headed north. Isaiah knew they were going toward Brandt's shop.

Brandt asked, "What the hell were you doing in a bank?

Isaiah answered, "Looking for a job."

Brandt snarled, "Looking for a job, hell. I'll give you a damn job. You'll wish like hell you never came anywhere near St. Louis."

They rushed Isaiah across the street and into Brandt's shop. Brandt took him down the hallway to a small room without any windows and gave him another belt behind the head before locking the door.

Isaiah rubbed the back of his head and thought that was the same kind of treatment that Tanner had to endure his entire life. It wasn't the pain that bothered him; it was the realization that his brother had to go through such senseless and degrading abuse.

Isaiah knew that Brandt would probably talk to Greenlee soon. Isaiah expected he could end up at Greenlee's before the day was over. He wondered if it would be advisable to tell Brandt who he was. Or would that get him killed? What about Alaina and Tanner? They were already talking to the sheriff;

with him missing, would they show up here looking for him? He decided to sit and quietly wait.

When the sheriff, Alaina, and Tanner entered the bank, they were attended to right away. After the sheriff inquired about Isaiah, Tanner, a bit later, asked. "Was Tom Brandt in the bank about that time?"

The teller smiled and said. "Why yes. Do you know Mr. Brandt? How in the world did you figure out that Mr. Brandt may be here?"

Tanner said to the sheriff. "We have to go right away."

The sheriff, Alaina, and Tanner crossed the street and were about to enter the shop when Tanner stopped them. A half block away, Art was sprinting in their direction. Tanner smiled, "Here comes Art."

The sheriff shook his head and dug in his pocket. Art arrived and immediately asked. "What happened? Where is Isaiah?"

Alaina explained. "Isaiah had to stop at the bank to see Manfred Martin. We couldn't stop him. We think Tom Brandt has him."

Without answering, Art reached for the door; the sheriff stopped him and said,. "Wait just a minute, Art. Put this deputy badge on and let me take the lead. We are going to arrest Brandt and see about getting Isaiah back."

The sheriff opened the door and was met by Brandt's henchman. As soon as he saw the sheriff's badge, one could see his guilt and fear. Art pushed his way in to stand beside the sheriff. The sheriff asked Tanner, "Tanner, do you recognize this man?"

Tanner nodded, "Yes, sir. We called him Mr. Lou; he was one of the guards."

Lou evidently was disquieted by seeing two of Tanner and then having this one called Tanner, who was the other one? Lou suddenly bolted down the hall. He made it about four steps before Art sent him sprawling on his face. Lou jumped up and was met by a solid black fist driven to his jaw. This time he was either dazed enough or smart enough to stay down.

Art took him by the shoulder, turned him over, and very icily asked. "Where is Brandt?"

Lou had enough of Art's closed fist, and the tone of his voice seemed to indicate that he would brook no hesitation. He nodded toward the closed door and said, "He's in the shop with the boys."

Art then asked, "Where is Tanner's brother?"

Lou replied down the hall in the room on the right. The boy is alright."

The sheriff put a pair of handcuffs on Lou. As Art went down the hall to check on Isaiah. The sheriff advised. "Art, wait. Don't make a lot of racket; we don't want to spook Brandt."

Art nodded that he understood; he realized what should be done; he tapped lightly on the door and quietly said, "Isaiah. It's Art."

Isaiah responded, "Art. I knew you'd come. Where's Tanner?"

Art smiled at Isaiah's interest in Tanner and informed him, "Tanner is here with me and Alaina. We are going to arrest Brandt and then get the key to the door. We'll have you out shortly."

The sheriff withdrew his sidearm and opened the shop door; Tanner was right behind him. There were three boys in the shop along with Brandt. The sheriff raised his pistol and said, Tom Brandt. You are under arrest. Keep your hands where I can see them and don't move."

When Art approached Brandt, he was about to put the handcuffs on when Brandt pulled away. Art reacted with a roundhouse right fist. He knocked Brandt over one of the benches onto the floor. Before Brandt could move, Art had a handcuff on him. Art quietly said to him, "The sheriff kindly told you not to move."

Tanner looked at the sheriff; the sheriff was grinning. Tanner figured the sheriff liked Art's punch probably almost as much as he and Art liked it.

The sheriff then said to Alaina and Tanner. "I would like you to get the names of these boys and any other boys that were here. Also, where they came from, who took them off the orphan train, and if they knew of any others that were on the orphan train that were taken under questionable circumstances. Get any other information you can gather about any other kids that were here… I have people coming here pretty soon that will take care of these boys and get them to a home of some kind.

By the time they got Isaiah out of the locked room, two sheriff's deputies had arrived along with a doctor.

Art took the sheriff aside and explained. "Word can't get back to Greenlee; otherwise he'll either skip town or conceivably do away with some of the evidence. I think we have to act on him fairly quickly."

The sheriff admitted. "Yeah. We have enough evidence with the testimony of Tanner alone to hold Greenlee. I'll have Greenlee's business raided very shortly."

Art smiled. "That's great, sheriff, because I think that he has three kids there right now that have been enslaved for quite some time."

They were about to walk away when the sheriff stopped Art and very quietly said, "Art. I have to ask? How did it feel when your fist landed on Brandt's jaw?"

Art returned the sheriff's smile and said, "Sheriff, you can't imagine how good that felt. The next time I'm fishing trout with Tanner on that trout stream up in Denver, I'm going to explain to him how good that felt."

The sheriff patted him on the back and said,. "I just want you to know it even felt good to me. Let's get these guys into jail. By the way… do you want to keep that deputy badge when we raid Greenlee's shop?"

Art grinned as he took off the badge. "I've been telling the boys and Alaina to let the law take care of handing out justice. I liked smacking those two a bit too much. I think I'll take a pass unless you decide you need me."

The sheriff shook Art's hand and said, "If I need help talking to any of the workers, can I call on you?"

Art nodded, "I'll stay in contact with the boys and Alaina. We'll have to talk to you before we leave town to make sure you get all the evidence you want out of us."

The sheriff took the key and gave it to Alaina to open the door, meanwhile Tanner thought he heard Art mention his name and fishing. Tanner smiled and said to Art. "Who was it that said we should allow the sheriff and the authorities to do the confronting? When you popped him in the kisser, that sure looked like a confrontation to me."

Art laughed and replied, "Yeah, I told the sheriff I was giving up the deputy badge, smacking those two felt way too good."

Isaiah took Art's arm. "Art. Alaina, Come with us. I am going to introduce Alaina and Tanner to Manny. Would you believe his bank is only a couple blocks from here?"

They crossed the street and Isaiah led the way stepping out in front of everyone, obviously excited. Tanner smiled and said to Art. "Art. Isaiah is anxious to see Manny. He must be a great friend."

Art smiled knowingly, "Wait till you meet Manny. I wonder what he will say about two of you."

Tanner asked, "He's a nice man?"

Art nodded, "Some would say he's too good for this world. He sure doesn't fit the mold of most bankers. Some say a banker must be a pretty cold person. Some say that banks and bankers have a license to steal. If that's the case, Manny and Randolph Kristofferson should never have made good as bankers. Both were great people.

"Don't be surprised if you are greeted with a hug and a kiss. Manny has two daughters that are just as nice as their dad. Isaiah, I think, is very fond of the company of Sharon."

Tanner grinned, "He never mentioned Sharon."

Art smiled and added, "When the Randolph and Karen Kristofferson were killed, Manny and his family hurried to

Denver to help in the funerals and making sure the bank was handled properly. When Manny came back to St. Louis he offered to bring Isaiah back with him."

Tanner asked, "What about you?"

Art laughed, "Me too. Manny said he wanted someone to go fishing with and since I was a good cook, he would really like me to come along. St. Louis is a great area to fish in. Yes Tanner, you'll like Manny and I think you'll like Susan too."

"Susan?"

Art grinned, "She's a very nice young gal. Sixteen. A lot like her father."

Tanner grinned and answered, "Is she going to welcome us with a hug and a kiss too?"

Art smiled at Tanner's question, "Very well could be. Be prepared."

For the next three days they remained in St. Louis assisting in contacting the one's knowledgeable of those hurt by Brandt and Greenlee. Because of his friends in St. Louis, Art was called on several times to help gather evidence on Greenlee. The judge placed the Greenlee factory in receivership because the charges against him included murder.

In those three days, they spent time with Manny and his family. Tanner learned that Manny's daughter Sharon and Isaiah were very comfortable in each other's presence, and he discovered that Susan was indeed a warm and affectionate person, much like her father and mother.

Part IV
Homecoming.
On the railroad heading for Westchester, Ill.
Friday June 20, 1879

Alaina sat facing Tanner and Isaiah; she smiled and said, "You boys have been pretty quiet."

Both smiled and nodded. Tanner explained. "It is a bit scary. It's something we've both thought about perhaps all our lives. Something we dreamed of. Isaiah and I have talked a lot about it. We've come to the conclusion we should be prepared for the worst."

Alaina asked, "You mean if your parents are deceased?"

Tanner shook his head. "That would be very sad, but we both recognize death is a possibility and something we should be prepared for. We think… what would be the worst… that is, we could be denied. That would be the worst."

Tanner smiled and added. "The best would be if there is a family of six or ten other sets of twins to get to know."

Isaiah nodded, "We've talked about just ignoring the farmer that sold Tanner to Brandt. Knowing now that there were a lot of people like him that were treating orphans very badly, selling them or giving them away. Then again, his poor behavior should be somehow addressed. For both of us, he isn't a pressing concern. Just think about how much we accomplished in St. Louis. I think, that is, we are hoping that everyone will be more watchful when it comes to the lives of orphan train kids."

Tanner nodded, “In other words, as we get closer to Kane County, the farmer that sold me isn’t our main concern.”

Alaina asked, “So you feel you are up to whatever happens?”

Tanner nodded, “Yes. I have Isaiah, and now I have Art, and you, Alaina.”

Isaiah added, “And, back in Denver, there is a gal by the name of Mary Jane Tremble that Tanner speaks well of.”

Tanner grinned, “And we’ve discovered that St. Louis isn’t so far away, so Isaiah can always see Sharon Martin now and then.”

Isaiah smiled, admitting to his attraction to Sharon. Alaina asked, “How long have you known Sharon?”

Isaiah smiled; one could see he was fond of Sharon. “We wrote to each other. Nearly every summer they made trips to Denver. Art and I and Sharon and Susan used to do a little fishing. We practically grew up together.”

Tanner added a little jibe, “There couldn’t be a much better place to grow up together than on the banks of that fishing hole.”

Isaiah returned with a little observation of his own. “I noted that you spent a bit of time with Susan.”

Tanner grinned and asked, “Does Susan like to fish?”

Art was grinning as he added, “This summer it could get a bit more interesting on the banks of the fishing hole.”

Alaina advised, “Tanner, in a couple days you will be eighteen. Take your time with fishing and with finding someone to share your life with.”

Tanner merely nodded his head and smiled seemingly in agreement.

Art smiled and added, “Getting back to the potential reunion, I think you both are taking a very healthy approach to this. And you are right. You can lean on us. You can fall back on a lot of friends and acquaintances that you’ve both made. I may add that the reason that you two have a lot of good friends is because you are both very well-behaved and welcoming boys. In short, you are good people.”

Alaina added, "I agree wholeheartedly. Boys, day after tomorrow, I will no longer be your guardian. You'll be on your own, but I want you to know, I'll only leave when you are comfortable with carrying on without me. And, who knows, maybe I'll join the three or five of you on the banks of that fishing stream.

Tanner grinned, "Thank you, Art and Alaina. And as Isaiah told me, 'We can always go home and dig out the fishing poles. Sitting on that fishing stream shore back home, I think that is about as healing and peaceful as life can get."

Alaina informed, "We are about an hour from Aurora. That is in Kane County. I think we should get a hotel room and then rent a carriage and do some inquiring about the location of the Gunnar and Louise Randolph home if they are still alive or in the area. And we can inquire about the Westchester orphanage while we are at it."

Art stopped a porter as he went by and asked, "Porter. I have a question. Are you familiar with Kane County?"

"Yes Sir. My home is in Aurora."

"Where is the county seat for Kane County?"

The porter didn't hesitate, "In Geneva."

Art asked, "Does the train stop there?"

"Yes, indeed. It is about fifteen miles past Aurora."

Art smiled and asked, "My brothers are Randolph's. Have you heard the name mentioned in Kane County?"

"No sir. But they should have records at the county seat in Geneva."

Art nodded, "That's very helpful. Thank you kindly."

Alaina smiled and asked, "Do they have a hotel in Geneva?"

The porter nodded, "Yes, ma'am. Nice hotel."

After a lengthy stop in Aurora, they made it to Geneva a little past closing time of the county seat. They checked in at the hotel and went to a local café to eat. While at the café, they inquired about the Randolph name with no success. After a walk around town inquiring, they retired to the hotel to wait until the county courthouse opened in the morning.

Alaina organized the next day. "We'll rent a carriage after breakfast in the morning. Of course, we'll ask a few more people about the Randolph name, and then we will go to the courthouse for official records. If we find nothing, we'll go to Westchester to the hospital and the orphanage to resume our search."

Remember boys, Sunday you will turn eighteen years old, and you can issue me my walking papers as your guardian at that time."

Tanner embraced Alaina and said, "We have a lot to thank you for. You'll never be issued any walking papers. Art said that Isaiah and I have a lot of people we can lean on. You can continue to watch over us as long as you want. You've been an amazing help. I'll be forever in your debt; you'll be forever in our thoughts."

Isaiah nodded his agreement and followed up with a hug of his own. He added, "Alaina, you've chosen a life of giving to those less fortunate. I thank you and wish you happiness and, most of all, safety when you get back home. Remember, you can always spend time with us in Denver; that trout stream is about the most peaceful place in the world."

On the road to Compton Hills.
6 miles from Geneva, Ill.
Saturday, June 21, 1879

Louise Randolph was hoeing in her garden when the buggy pulled into her yard. She smiled and asked, "Jimmy Bradley, what in the world gets you up so early in the morning?"

Jim got down and stretched his legs and tossed the reins over the hitching rail before he answered, "Louise, it's going on eleven o'clock. I thought I'd drop by for a cup of coffee and maybe warn you in case the creditors are after you."

Louise laughed heartily, "I've almost accumulated enough so that in another few years someone may feel what I have is worthwhile enough to take if I was in debt."

Jim laughed as they headed to the house, "Are you still helping to raise the neighbor's children?"

"Now and then. Most of them have grown up. I still do a little sewing for the Anderson clan and quilting for the store in Aurora. I stay busy."

"Louise, how long has it been since Gunnar passed away?"

"Close to ten years."

Louise poured Jim's coffee, then sat down and asked, "Now what is the real reason I get the pleasure of your visit?"

Jim smiled, "I bumped into Dick Gregor over in St. Charles. Boy, that little burg is growing."

Louise asked, "What did Dick have to say?"

Jim shrugged. "This is about third-hand information. Dick talked to some guy by the name of Wiley, who was over in Geneva last night. He said there was a gal, a Black guy, and a pair of kids asking about the Randolph name. He said that he may have heard the name Gunnar and maybe Louise. He said since I talked about you a couple of times, maybe you should know."

Louise shook her head. “Well, Jim, I don’t have any outstanding debts worth pursuing but you said there was a pair of kids asking also?”

Jim smiled and laughed, “Yeah. Wiley said, He was told you couldn’t tell the two boys apart.”

Louise’s face became very serious. “You couldn’t tell them apart. They were twins?”

Jim shrugged, “That’s what it sounded like. Wiley said they were going to inquire at the county seat in Geneva this morning about the whereabouts of anyone in Kane County by your name. They just may be on the way out to see you sometime today.”

Jim was alarmed at the look on Louise’s face. “Louise. Are you all right?”

Louise picked up a fan and fanned her face; she shook her head in disbelief and hope. Very seriously suddenly, she related, “My goodness, Jim. Most people don’t know. When Gunnar and I settled here, we decided to start having children. When I was almost due, Gunnar broke his back. Without any income, we decided to give up the child. There were two babies, twins. We named them Tanner and Isaiah and agreed to turn them over to the Westchester Orphanage. I was told they didn’t even make it out of the hospital. They were adopted. They never gave us the details. That’s the way they did things at that time. We had no choice but to walk away. With Gunnar laid up with a broken back, it would have been impossible to raise them. As it was, the first five years was touch and go whether or not we’d be able to keep our home.”

Jim shook his head and said, “Louise. That set of twins could be your babies.”

Louise wagged her head in astonishment and said,. “Tomorrow those boys, if they are my boys, they will be eighteen.”

Louise. I can’t imagine what is going through your mind right now.”

She closed her eyes and related. “Everything. Fear, hope, memories, joy…

“Since Gunnar broke his back, like I said, we almost lost everything. We had so little… I was able to keep us afloat while caring for Gunnar.” She shook her head. “The memories… I have beaten up on myself many times over the years… but we never would have been able to raise the boys. You know...” Her voice trailed off at the recollection of all they went through.

Jim interjected, “So Gunnar was an invalid for…”

“Nine… almost ten years…”

Jim shook his head. “I’ll repeat what a few neighbors have said: You are one amazing woman, Louise.”

“Thank you, Jim. Right now I guess I just feel anticipation. My mind is a whirlwind of thoughts. It all may turn out to be nothing but hope. Maybe I should go back out and hoe the garden.”

Jim laughed and rose. “I suppose I better get home and hug my bride; she will think I stopped to go fishing.”

As they walked out to the garden, Louise added, “Fishing. Jim, when Gunnar was bedridden, he always used to say that he wished he was on the way to take Isaiah and Tanner fishing. I told him that would happen someday in the great beyond. That always brought a smile to his face.”

About the time that Jim got his rig ready to go, a buggy was seen coming up the road. Art could be easily seen in the front seat driving the rig. Jim said. “Good lord Louise, this could be them. Maybe I’ll stick around for a minute.”

Louise couldn’t talk; she held her hand to her mouth as the rig turned into her driveway. Jim said, “If they are your twins, you’ll have to learn their names.”

Louise calmly removed her hand from her mouth and smiled, “No. I’ll know their names.”

Jim laughed as though she were telling a joke as the buggy pulled up to the hitching rail. Identical twins stepped out of the buggy. With big smiles on their faces they hurried to her. Tanner said, “Mom?”

With nothing else said she held out her arms and embraced the two of them; there were a lot of tears shed, including Jim's,

Art's and Alaina's. Finally Jim said, "I told Louise someone would have to introduce you two, but she said she would know you by name."

Louise turned Isaiah's head to the side, not knowing why, Isaiah still submitted to the gentle push. Their mother said, "This one is Isaiah; this one is Tanner."

Tanner exclaimed, "Mom! How did you figure that out?"

Louise Randolph smiled and said, "There is a tiny birthmark in back of Isaiah's left ear. I held you two for three days before I had to leave you behind. That birthmark was how I kept track of you two."

She kissed them, cried a bit at the memory, when drying her eyes Isaiah asked. "According to the records, Dad died about nine years ago."

Louise nodded, "Yes. Almost ten years ago. Your dad broke his back when I was eight months pregnant. He was bedridden for almost nine years before he passed away. Boys, your dad did a lot of daydreaming; he always talked about wishing he was fishing with you two boys. We so much wished we could have kept you both, but we almost lost everything as it was."

She took them in her arms again and then said. "This man with the tears in his eyes is my good neighbor Jim Bradley. Now, can you introduce me to these two people you are with?"

After handshakes with Jim, Tanner made the introductions. "This gentleman, Isaiah and I refer to as our big brother, his name is Art. He has been with the family as long as Isaiah. I think Gunnar, our father, sent him to us so that Art could take us fishing. Art is a great fisherman and as nice as any brother could be. He's a very talented man, and we are lucky he sticks with us.

"And, when we talk about nice people, this is Alaina. She is our guardian, but mostly she is our friend and lifesaver. We think we have her to thank for getting the two of us, and now all of us together."

Louise gave Art a hug and said, "Thank you, Art, for all the trust the boys have in you. And Alaina. I'm sure the boys will tell me all about both of you. It sounds like you've both been very important people in their lives.

Jim announced, "I'm leaving; I'm running late. I want you all to know that everyone in the neighborhood respects this lady; she has helped a lot of families in the area over the past 18 years in many ways."

Louise ordered, "Tie up your horse; let's go in the house. I have a feeling there is a lot of catching up that we have to do."

Louise took the arms of Isiah and Tanner and led them to the house. She asked, "Tell me, boys. Are there going to be a lot of happy tales, or do I need to get out a crying towel?"

Tanner smiled and said, "Mom. I'm afraid that you'll get a little of both, but the best, the happiest tales, those I think we are going to create from here on."

Epilogue

An Epilogue is meant to inform what is missed, forgotten or inadvertently left out. For my purpose I'll summarize information related to my story telling. What has the errant youth of my Jack Pine Savage days and the extended stay at the Wisconsin Child Center produced in my writing?

I hope it was evident there is a seeking of kindness, equity, and fair play, sometimes with a rather harsh justice. You may have seen some aloofness, independence, and perhaps some defiance in the characters.

Because of the complete lack of support for our family during my childhood, I have established a strong belief in some of our social institutions; public education, affordable health care, Medicare, and social security. I believe these programs are the cement that holds society together, gives dignity to all and helps to pick us up when we stumble.

Regarding government, my favorite quote comes from Thomas Jefferson, "Government's one job is the best interests of the people." I would add to that quote; young families should be the government's priority. I hold parents, foster parents, adoptive parents, in the highest regard; family is everything. I feel the government's main job should be to help young families to thrive.

I often consider the judge's meanness to my mother in that very short courtroom hearing that established my fate away from birth family from age eleven on. His sudden biased decision with prejudice toward my mother's plight has established in me prejudice of my own. Now, when laws or decisions are handed out that are not in the best interest of society, I feel the need to speak up. I also feel more people should voice their opinions. I feel it is society that must put a face on laws, if the law, or its execution fails to be in the best interest of the people; we all need to speak out.

Sometimes now I scribble to speak out, sometimes I just scribble. The following is posted on a wall in my rec room. To quote me:

"The evolution of man speaks of family, bonding, companionship, acceptance, community, love.... It is through letters, prose, poem, artistry and song that we can forever share our love and a suggestion of who we are with the world."

In regard to family and friends, I carried the following scribbling in my wallet for many years as a message to whoever happens to be present at my; 'final' time.

It is said the Methuselah tree is about 5000 years old; there are other bristlecone pine trees up to 7000 years old. Sooner or later all living things die and are returned to the earth as fuel for other living things. The sadness is; the tree, no matter the eons, will experience nothing. We humans live a shorter but more joyous life in close companionship with friends, parents, siblings, and, if we are lucky, a partner, children, grand-children, great grandchildren.... If my "time" arrives, don't fret, rather consider, I have been blessed, you have added the comfort of your companionship to my life's experience.

I read the preceding note to a great gentleman friend, Vince Capozzi at nearly one-hundred-years old a few days before he passed away. In my visits during the weeks prior to his passing, he frequently spoke about the importance of companionship in our lives, upon my reading the note, Vince responded, "That's exactly how I feel."

When I consider my scribbling, life, hobbies, the ageing process; beyond family, what is important? To my estimation,

Mahatma Gandhi's simple statement melts down a key to a healthy mankind, "Everybody understands kindness."

Hangdog

Introduction:

Of all the stories of orphan train children that tug at one's heartstrings, the instances' whereby orphaned siblings are separated are particularly painful. The potential adopting parents often are reluctant to take on more than one child at a time. As a child, to be removed from the home and then having brothers or sisters permanently taken away can inflict a forever pain.

One true tale of three orphan train riders goes something like this. Mom dies; the father then puts the three boys on the orphan train; the person in charge of the train steals the envelope with their father's address, then admonishes the boys not to think of the past. When the youngest, a four-year-old, is 'picked,' he is carried away while screaming for his 'brovers'. A few stops later, the middle brother is selected; the oldest, who eventually tells the tale, is all alone. Later, as an adult, although he searches, he never sees his brothers or their father again.

In the story, Hangdog, the pain of the oldest and perhaps the most aware and in this instance, sensitive, considers it her responsibility to keep the sisters together after their parent's death. She has been promised that the girls will be taken to a new home together; however, she justifiably has little trust in her alleged uncle. The imposter poses as their uncle intends on stealing the money from their estate and abandoning them.

In this story their luck changes because of a couple of unrelated strangers.

It is said that one cannot judge a book by its cover; I would say that the same saying could be said about the looks of people.

The origin of this book's title came from my friend Dr. Marvin Lansing. The idea and the title, 'Hangdog,' makes me grin.

When working as an educator, I was put on the negotiating team. Sometime later, I was moved up to the board office. The superintendent, Dr. Marvin Lansing, spoke to me and talked of my "hangdog" expression. I didn't know what he was talking about.

Later, I spoke to friends and related the story; they laughed and indicated that anyone who negotiated across the table with Marv said he had a hangdog expression. I asked other friends who said that when I was negotiating, they said they were glad they were on the same side of the negotiating table.

When researching the hangdog expression, I came up with a sad or sorrowful expression. When I and others talk of the hangdog expression most people think of a very serios look. When across the table, both Marv and I had that same intent serious look, the "hangdog" look.

Marv also had a propensity to cuss now and then. In this story, I've added a bit of cursing in memory of Marv.

Growing up Marv and I both had a few bumps, bruises, and perhaps a few more challenges in our lives than most. In some ways those hurdles we had to overcome were part of what shaped our lives, our personality, our philosophy and who knows, perhaps even a reason for our 'hangdog' look.

One's ‘look’ can be deceiving. I had a friend; I figured he was the most stern-looking person I've ever met. He knew he had a rather fearsome look and used his ‘look’ as a joke whenever possible. The first time I met him; I asked him a simple question. He snapped his head to me and uttered a loud, Huh? I was shocked; he laughed at my reaction. It turned out he was a very great and funny guy.

Where did I get the idea and appreciation for the hero’s memory for names and its impact on people? Besides being a good negotiator, as the superintendent, Marv had the gift of an encyclopedic memory for names of the staff, and their families. That recall ability personalized Marv’s contacts with everyone. Currently, some 35 years after retiring, Marv still retained much of that ability to recall names.

When mentioning the ability to recall names/ another individual that had an amazing memory for names and deserves mentioning was my foster father, Sam Hagerman. One year Sam was asked to be a part of the La Crosse Octoberfest Parade as Parade Marshal. That first year, from the float, he belted out the names of many of the people on the entire parade route. From that year on, Sam Hagerman was the Octoberfest Parade Marshal.

Hangdog

July 17, 1869

The Chicago West Side Railroad Station was busy, which suited the man known to the three girls only by the first name, Frank. With the girls he was stern and aloof; they feared him so much that they couldn't ask questions. Now, he ordered the girls to sit and wait.

Bewildered and still in shock after the sudden deaths of their mother and father, the three girls huddled together on the bench and obeyed. After losing their mother and father in a horrible accident, their hope was the promise that Frank made to them. He promised the girls and their neighbors that the three of them would remain together. The oldest, ten-year-old Audrey had doubts.

For Frank, this all started when he came to Chicago after he saw that a man and a woman had been killed and left three children without any known relatives. Upon investigating, Frank learned there was a house and property he could claim and sell if he could pose as a brother to the father. He had the proceeds of the sale of the property in his pocket, now he had to sell or ditch the girls.

Frank studied the people in the train station carefully; he wanted to try to give the girls away or sell them, and he was running out of time. When he lied about being the father's brother, he promised that he had a good home for them. Now he had to get himself and the girls far enough away from Chicago so nobody would check up on him. There were a lot of orphan kids running around on the streets; the neighbors wanted assurance that the three girls would go to a good home.

He mulled over his bad luck; the disposition of the three girls was going to be more difficult than he thought. Now he planned on putting them on the train as far as Naperville, then he would jump off at a stop before getting there and leave the girls behind as someone else's problem.

He figured he had a good deal cooking; he convinced the Constable that he was the girl's uncle. After being paid for the house and everything that he could sell, he made out pretty good. Over $300—that was a good deal of money. He figured the longer he kept them with him, the more of that money would disappear. He thought his best plan would be to put them on the train, and halfway to their destination, he would leave the train and let somebody else figure out what to do with the three girls.

As he sat with the three girls next to the ticket counter pondering his move, a man walked past him to pick up his ticket. He was well-dressed, but Frank discounted him because, at first glance, he looked like he may be a bit ornery. Frank figured he needed a soft touch; this guy looked like he would be tough to deal with.

Frank turned away; however, when the guy got to the ticket counter, the ticket salesperson addressed him warmly. With a smile he announced, "Hangdog! I haven't seen you in six months. I suppose you have a bucket of that Denver gold mine of yours with you in that satchel."

At the mention of gold, Frank became very attentive. When the man called Hangdog responded, he spoke quietly and was not heard by Frank. Frank was impressed when 'Hangdog' hoisted a very heavy-looking satchel onto the counter. Hangdog and the ticket seller spoke amiably for some time before another customer came up.

Frank watched the man called Hangdog as he sat on a bench with the very heavy satchel on one side of him and another lighter satchel on the other side. Frank figured the stranger got the name Hangdog by the serious look on his face.

Considering that heavy satchel in possession of the gold mine owner, in Frank's mind, his plans were now being modified. Now his plan included that satchel of gold. Frank stood and spoke to the oldest of the three girls, "Andrea. Keep the little ones out of mischief."

Audrey gave him a cool look and said, "I am Audrey. The little one is Alanna."

Frank snapped back. "Whatever. Watch her!"

Frank went to the ticket counter; his plans changed when gold was mentioned, and the heavy satchel was seen. "I noticed that you called that guy Hangdog, from his looks he got the name honestly."

The salesclerk smiled and explained. "Yeah. I was happy to see him; I spoke a bit too loud. His name is Carl Cromwell. About the nicest man in the world, but you are right. Until he smiles, he wears a Hangdog look on his face. I met him six months ago, and he still remembered my name, and he asked how my son is doing with his arm. My son had just broken his arm when he came here the last time. Great guy with a great memory. What can I do for you?"

Frank was almost drooling thinking of the heavy satchel of gold. He answered," I just need tickets for the three girls and myself to Naperville."

As the clerk got the tickets, Frank asked, "You mentioned he had a gold mine?"

The clerk nodded. "Have you heard of the Denver Cromwell mine?"

Frank nodded. "Oh yeah. Quite an operation."

The clerk put the tickets on the counter and replied, "Yes. Carl was a lucky one."

Frank paid for the tickets and went and sat with the three girls with a calculating grin on his face. He figured maybe he could get rid of the girls while making a lot more money than he already had if he got his hands on that satchel.

Alanna pulled at his sleeve and spoke. "I have to go potty."

Summoned back to reality, Frank lost his smile. "Andrea. Take her to the bathroom."

Frank's mind was on that satchel; he was oblivious to the cold stare in return. "I am Audrey. This is Alanna."

Frank's mind was on the satchel filled with gold; he merely grumbled. "Whatever."

Frank was busy plotting his getaway with the satchel. There was this station and two other towns where he could make it happen. As soon as he can get Hangdog away from the satchel, at either of the three places, he would grab the satchel. His timing would have to include the actual startup of the train so that he could jump off the train and get away without pursuit.

Alanna and Audrey returned, and an announcement was made to board the train. Frank ordered. "Kids. Stay with me now. Andrea, hang onto the little one." This time Audrey didn't even respond.

Frank was determined to stage his entry onto the train so that he would be as close to Hangdog as possible.

As they walked out the door, Frank stayed close behind Hangdog. Frank's mind could only recall the nickname. As they entered the rail car, Frank remained close behind, thinking that the best scenario was to grab the satchel as the train pulled out of the station. It would be easy to get lost quickly in Chicago and the girls may not be checked up on until they arrive at their destination in Naperville.

Carl Cromwell was tired; he was glad he purchased a sleeping berth for the nights, it was a long trip to Denver. For now, he would get in a booth, put his feet on his satchels, close his eyes, and relax. He slid over to the window; there was room for an adult beside him and a bench seat facing him that would hold two people. He closed his eyes and considered the busy day before that got him so tired.

When Carl came to Chicago, he wanted to merely purchase tile samples for his oldest daughter, Crystal, who was interested in enlivening her kitchen and bathrooms and being able to sell tile to others in the Denver area. In the process of selecting tile, he ended up purchasing the tile company. He smiled at the thought.

With his eyes closed before sleep overtook him, he could hear movement in the booth with him. His eyes opened and closed; he glimpsed what appeared to be a young family of three girls in the booth with him.

As sleep gradually overtook him, he figured if his daughter Crystal didn't like the tile samples currently in production, she could design and manufacture her own.

Frank noted that the man called Hangdog kept the heavy satchel close to him. He no more than sat down before he put his feet on the satchel and closed his eyes. At first Frank thought, this is going to be easier than I thought. Maybe I can get off the train right here in Chicago.

Frank gave Alanna a gentle push into the booth next to the one he referred to as Hangdog. Karl quietly ordered. "Sit and be quiet."

Frank sat next to Alanna and ordered. You two sit across from us and be quiet." Frank wanted Hangdog in a deep sleep.

When the train started to move, Frank glanced at the satchel and Hangdog he was about to make grab the satchel. For a moment Hangdog opened his eyes, then closed them. Frank figured he'd better wait till the next stop and find some way to separate Hangdog from his gold.

In the little town of Downers Grove, the next stop for the railroad, that morning when Krystal Kenworth woke up, she was determined to do something different about her life. She knew the family doctor would be in his office early getting ready for his patients. Since the doctor was also a close friend, she would just barge in on him before he normally took patients. She went to the back door, knocked, and walked in.

Dr. Ernest Longwell turned from his desk and smiled, "Krystal. Please come right in. To what do I owe this pleasure?"

Without humor, she was blunt, "Ernie. I need either some very strong pills or some real good advice."

The good doctor and friend guessed. "Still feeling despondent over the loss of your husband and son?"

Krystal sat down, nodded, and explained. "Some, of course, but Ernie. I wake up in the same bed. I work way too many hours, so I don't have to go home. I can't stand being in the house. I can't stand everyone in the town no matter their good intentions as they constantly remind me of the past forcing me to dwell on my loss."

Again, the doctor made a guess. "Too many memories."

Krystal nodded." Yes. Also, in this small town of Downers Grove, nobody will leave me be… Everyone feels sorry for me, and they won't let me forget and move on. They won't let me go on with my life."

The doctor shook his head. "That damn war should never have happened. Brother fighting brother over the right to enslave people. I told your son not to go. He felt he had to follow his dad's lead."

Krystal shook her head at the memory and asked. "Are you going to give me some advice or some powerful medication?"

The doctor shook his head. "I'm not going to give you any damn pills, but as a friend, I will give you some advice. A train leaves here this morning heading west. Go home, pack a small bag or two, get on the train, and get the hell out of town. Get away. The train goes all the way to California."

Krystal responded. "What about the house, the business…"

"That is what you are fighting. After you've packed a bag or two, leave the house open. I'll take care of it. Same goes with your store. You have good people there working for you; don't worry about it. I'll look into it. Go to the damn bank on your way to the rail station and take out enough to get you to California and back."

Krystal thought the idea of getting away actually appealed to her. "What about..."

The doctor smiled and interrupted, "The hell with worrying. Krystal… Go! Get out of here. Go, find a reason to laugh again. Hell; find reasons to laugh out loud! Find people you thoroughly enjoy being with. Hell, maybe even fall in love again or at least find reasons to love. You are a wonderful person. Here you are 43 years old! You have a lot of life ahead of you. You are a talented person. Find a purpose. Find someone that is just as nice as you are."

Krystal put her head down and thought that much of what Ernie said made sense. What could a trip to California and back hurt?

Ernie asked. "So, what the hell are you waiting for?"

Krystal stood and offered her hand; Ernie embraced her and spoke. "Krystal. You have always been a talented, wonderful, outgoing lady. Go find that person. Write to me if you need anything. And Krystal. Do you recall when John Beck's wife passed away five or ten years ago?"

Sure, I do. Her name was Felicity. John is a very nice man."

The doctor smiled, "Joy liked to be called Felicity, her name was Joy. Felicity means Joy. John related to me not too long ago that he had gained many more friends. He said that without Joy, he is now initiating conversations with people, and he is very happy with everyone's response, he is finding there is a lot of great people out there.. He has made a lot more friends. So, Krystal, don't be afraid to reach out, and dammit, with a smile."

Krystal turned to go, she related, "Well, I just hope I can return a smile now and then."

As Krystal left the office, she felt a bit liberated already. At least she got an, okay to get away. The bank was right around the corner; she picked up a thousand dollars; she could get to California and back a couple of times.

The bank teller was surprised at the amount, he questioned, "Krystal. What are you going to do with all that money?"

Krystal almost wanted to tell him it was none of his business, however she related, "Don't tell anyone. I'm going to bury it in the back yard for safekeeping."

She informed the bank that she would be away for some time, and they would continue paying her workers. If there was any change, she would inform them.

It seemed to Krystal that her burden was a bit lighter when she left the bank. She hailed Edna as she was about to enter her store. The store was another place she wanted to get away from. "Edna!"

She ran to catch up with Edna and related. "I won't be in for a while. The bank will continue to issue paychecks. You are in charge. I will contact you in a few days to see how everything is going."

Edna was obviously surprised. "This is pretty sudden."

Krystal nodded. "Yes. I was thinking that this will give you an opportunity to manage the business. And, who knows? I may decide to sell the business after all."

In the past Edna had expressed interest in purchasing the business, Krystal thought this would give her an opportunity to see if that interest was warranted.

Krystal got away quickly from Edna to stave off any conversation attempting to delve into why and blaming it on the loss of her husband and son. She continued to walk rapidly to her house, avoiding people and feeling good about her pending departure. When or if she returned, she hoped the pain and the constant reminder of the loss of her husband and son would be behind her.

She wondered at her friend the doctor's advice: learn to smile again, laugh out loud. Both seemed like a long way off but for now her burden did seem a bit lessened.

On the train, when Carl awoke, he felt a presence beside him; he glanced down at the smallest of the three girls. There was space between her and who he assumed was their father. He looked across the booth at the other two girls; the middle one seemed to be consoling the oldest one. None of the three girls looked the least bit happy; there seemed to be no joy, no seeking fun, not even a bit of mischief in any of them.

Frank got up to run an errand of some sort; Alanna moved a little closer to Clay. Clay looked down at Alanna and spoke. "Hi. I am Clay. What's your name?"

Alanna's face lit up as she answered. "I'm Alanna."

Clay smiled at her happy response. "Alanna, what are your sister's names?"

Alanna pointed and informed. "That's Andrea. That's Audrey."

"Where is your dad taking you girls?"

Alanna shook her head. 'He's not our dad. He's taking us some place to be with a family. Mom and Dad died."

Clay put his arm around Alanna and said." I'm so sorry to hear that. So, you are on your way to a good home. That's good."

Andrea spoke up. "Frank said he is taking us to a good home where we can all be together."

Clay nodded. "Yes. Being together is very important. You can help each other when you are hurt or feeling bad or just having fun playing together".

Clay looked at Andrea when he spoke; Andrea smiled. After comforting Audrey, she felt as though his admonishment was directed at her, it made her feel good.

Alanna looked up at Clay, smiled, and said, "My mom would call you a sleepyhead."

Andrea's and Audrey's eyes opened wide, and they were about to admonish Alanna when Clay burst out laughing and explained. "It won't be long, and I may be going to take another nap. I was up most of the night. I didn't get much sleep."

Alanna asked." Why did you stay up all night?"

Clay chuckled. "I was in a hurry to get done so I could get on the train to go home, so I spent the night making a purchase."

Andrea asked. "It took you all night to buy something. What did you buy?"

Clay again laughed at the question. “I bought a factory.” Clay thought Andrea was a pretty smart young lady, her question showed a natural inquisitiveness.

Clay looked at Andrea and spoke. “Andrea, before you get off this train, I’m going to purchase some pencils and paper for you. I want you to write me a letter now and then. I think you girls are very nice and sharp young ladies.”

Audrey was wondering what happened to Frank. He promised to keep them together. He promised... He said he knew of a wonderful couple that wanted three children; then they were all put on a train with very few clothes... Audrey was near panic; she wanted the three girls to remain together, and now that all depended on Frank. Audrey wondered, could she trust Frank? She felt the burden of keeping them together was mainly her responsibility since she was the oldest.

Audrey quietly observed the conversation between Alanna and the stranger. When Alanna mentioned her mom and dad had died, the stranger put his arm around her to comfort her. Audrey was near tears as she realized that when the stranger put his arm around Alanna, it was the first show of affection that was given to them after Mom and Dad had passed away.

Audrey observed as Alanna spoke with the sleepy stranger; she saw his face light up when Alanna called him a sleepyhead. She listened to the conversation with Andrea and thought that the stranger had a lot of compassion. The conversation was also very natural, with nothing hidden and no admonishment to limit or put down. She also thought that the stranger’s offer to purchase writing materials for Andrea showed friendliness, and an understanding and well-meaning closeness.

Audrey thought the stranger continued to hold Alanna, it seemed that the showing of warmth was a very natural part of him.

Again, Audrey shrank a bit, wondering where Frank was. Where was he taking them? Why didn’t he explain, why didn’t he talk? The train started to slow for the next stop. The conductor announced, “Downers Grove, this stop will be about 15 minutes.”

Audrey wondered, where was Frank? If he abandoned them, what would they do?

Frank had asked the conductor when the train was due to make the next stop; he had decided on a plan to separate Hangdog from that heavy satchel of gold. He got up and walked forward two cars and waited.

Krystal Kenworth was packed; she waited patiently on the bench outside the railroad station at Downers Grove. She could see the train approaching. She was committed to the idea of leaving Downers Grove and creating a change in her life. The doctor’s advice seemed to fit her needs of a way to solve her problem. She couldn’t stay, dwell and be constantly reminded of the past, she wanted to be a part of something or someone, that was not a constant reminder of her past.

As the train slowed down for boarding, she looked down at her two bags. She thought about packing while at her home that was filled with dishes and pots and pans, furniture, pictures, and memories of all sorts. For the time being, they were all left behind. For the time being, she would seek something different: as the doctor suggested: a smile, a laugh, laughter, the joy of a loving touch… companionship, love??

Krystal boarded the train, put her two bags on the seat next to her, and sat. She closed her eyes and wondered where her adventure would take her. Would she find reasons to smile, to laugh, or find a loving touch or… love? Even now she thought of what she was getting away from, it was like a constant cloud. Where was the sunshine?

Frank was now two cars forward of Clay and the girls. When Frank considered that the timing was right, he approached the conductor and asked, “You know the man they refer to as Hangdog two cars back?”

The conductor nodded. "Yes, Frank. I'm heading that way. His name is Clay."

Frank was a little disturbed by the fact that the conductor recalled his name, but he went on. "Would you tell him I need to speak to him? It's important. I'll be waiting right here."

The conductor shrugged. "Sure." The conductor wondered why Frank just didn't go back to his seat and talk to Clay himself. Puzzles were something the conductor, John Rothberg, had always been pretty good at solving.

As the train started to move, the conductor informed Clay. "Frank would like to talk to you. He is two cars forward. He said it was important."

Clay saw the quizzical and fear-like look on Audrey's face; for some reason, he felt it necessary to reassure all three girls. "I will be back. I won't be gone long. Stay together; I won't be gone long."

Meanwhile, Frank got off the slow-moving train. He walked back close to the side of the cars and quickly got back to the boarding spot just behind the booth where the satchel was.

Audrey was sitting near the window; she wondered why Frank wanted to talk to Clay. Audrey glanced out the window and thought she saw Frank's back. A few seconds later, Frank entered the car; he quickly reached down and grabbed the heavy bag of Clay's. Without a word to the girls, he turned and left. The next thing Audrey saw out the window was Frank running away with Clay's bag, and the train was picking up speed.

Audrey's worst fears suddenly became real. Frank had left them alone. They had no idea where Frank was taking them. He must have planned on leaving them.

The conductor, John Rothberg was now two cars back of the booth where the girls and Clay were seated. He glanced out the window and saw Frank running back toward him with Clay's bag in his hand. He realized Frank had intentionally lured Clay away from his bags. The conductor quickly opened the gate, stepped off the train, and met Frank with a small .32 caliber pistol. The train was starting to pick up speed as the conductor ordered. "Frank. Get back on the train."

Once on the train, the conductor took Clay's bag and ordered Frank to empty his pockets. The conductor reached inside Frank's vest and removed a thick wallet. The train continued to pick up speed.

They were between two railcars, two cars behind Clay and the girls. The conductor told Frank to turn around and face the outside. He read the information in the wallet as he apprised Frank. "Let's see. One Franklin Dickerson. Hmmm…Franklin, keep your hands up where I can see them. Franklin, I want you to know I was a Chicago cop before I took on this job as conductor. Thank you for giving me a reminder of why I hated that job. Just about every day I ran into slime just like you."

The conductor read the information on the three girls and then added. "So, Franklin… You posed as the uncle to the three girls. Then you sold and took the 350 dollars from the sale of the house. Were you going to sell the kids too?"

"Don't bother answering, Franklin. I don't see how I could believe a word you said anyway. Franklin. I'll give you the opportunity to tell me the whole story, or I could just turn you around and shoot you between the eyes and drop you off the train."

For some time, Frank related exactly what he had done, filling in the blanks for the conductor, including what led to the idea of stealing the heavy satchel.

The conductor ordered, "Turn around and face me, Frank. Now back up and be careful so you don't fall off the train. I'm going to give you two options, Frank. You can take option one or option two, and I'm not giving you long to decide which option you decide to take. The train is now going about 30 to 40 miles an hour. If you take one step backward, you will fall off the train. Here are your options Frank. Option one. I shoot you, and you fall off the train. Option two, I count to two; if you haven't jumped off the train, then you will automatically accept option number one. Remember option one is: I shoot you, and you fall off the train."

The gun was leveled at Frank's nose. "To make sure you understand your options; explain them to me."

Frank sensed that the conductor would have no reluctance about pulling the trigger; actually, Frank sensed that the conductor wanted to shoot him. Frank said, "I either jump or get shot."

The conductor grinned and then said loudly, "Very good, Frank. Remember there won't be much time between one and two. Are you ready?! One!"

Frank quickly dove off the train as the conductor said two, and the 32 special exploded.

The conductor picked up Clay's heavy bag and walked forward to return it.

Not finding Frank where he was supposed to be, Clay returned to find Audrey almost frozen with fear. Clay squeezed in between Andrea and Audrey and put his arm around Audrey and pulled her close. "Please, Audrey, tell me what's bothering you."

Audrey cried; she couldn't express her fears to the kind stranger, but Andrea explained. "She saw Frank running past the window, then Frank ran in and stole your bag and ran away. Audrey is very afraid of us three being broken up."

Now Andrea was near tears; Clay put his other arm around Andrea and declared. "All three of you listen carefully. Nobody is going to separate you. I will never leave you until you are all very happy, even if I must adopt all three of you myself."

Clay pulled Audrey a little closer and asked," Audrey, look at me, Audrey. We will get through this together. Do you believe me, Audrey?"

Audrey needed to believe Clay; she looked up at a smiling face that she was beginning to trust and nodded her head as Alanna crawled up to join them on Clay's lap. "Good. Whatever happens, you three will remain together, and I will not abandon you. You will be happy. If there is a problem at any time, please don't be afraid to ask; don't be afraid to talk about it.'

Alanna responded after giving Clay a hug," I have to go potty."

Clay chuckled. Andrea, can you take Alanna to the bathroom?"

Andrea's response seemed more than cautious. Clay recognized her reluctance to take her little sister to a place where there were a lot of adults. Clay turned around and saw Krystal. "Andrea. Would you ask that nice lady to help you? I know there are a lot of adults going in and out of there."

Krystal was busy watching the scenery go by when Andrea touched her arm and asked. "Alanna has to go to the bathroom. Could you come with us?"

Krystal didn't hesitate. "Why, surely."

Alanna smiled and took her hand; Krystal was warmed by being needed for the simple task and even the touch of the little girl. She wondered why she was asked, other than being the only single available adult close by. There had been quite a bit of activity in the booth where the girls were seated, and she recognized there wasn't a mother present. The father seemed a bit older, she asked. "Alanna. Where are you girls going?"

Alanna shrugged and replied." We don't know yet."

Andrea explained. "Frank said he was our uncle. He stole Clay's bag and ran away. Frank said he was our uncle, but I think he lied. Frank sold our house and everything. Clay is a nice man, he said he would keep us together even if he had to adopt us."

Krystal was amazed at what she was hearing. With a reputation for always being a good businesswoman and problem solver, questions piled up in her mind. After taking care of Alanna, on the way back to their car, she asked, "Clay is a friend of the family?"

Andrea shook her head. "No. We just met Clay on the train. He's a very nice man."

Alanna, still hanging onto Krystal's hand, added, "Clay said he will not abandon us. What does abandon mean?"

Andrea answered, "That means he will stay with us. He won't leave us."

Alanna looked up to Krystal. "I like Clay. He's funny."

More questions piled up in Krystal's mind. When they got back to the booth, Andrea invited her to join them. "Do you want to meet Clay?"

Krystal did want to meet Clay; she wanted answers to a lot of questions about the proper determination of the future of the three girls. "I would like to meet Clay, and what is your sister's name?"

"Audrey. I think Audrey is still afraid that we will be left alone or broken up. Now Clay is trying to reassure her."

Andrea slid in next to Clay and introduced. "This is Clay."

Clay smiled and said, "I'm Clay Cromwell. I'm sorry for having to impose on you. Please have a seat. You met Andrea and Alanna. This is Audrey. The girls lost their mom and dad a while ago... so we are in the process of healing. And what is your name?"

"Krystal Kenworth."

Clay smiled and said, "My goodness, I have a daughter named Crystal. My Crystal has two little children."

Just then the conductor arrived with Clay's bag. He sat down next to Krystal and greeted. "Clay, Krystal, and girls. This will take a moment, and the news isn't good. By the way, Clay, what in the world was Frank stealing that is so heavy?"

Clay smiled and answered with his arm still around Audrey. "It is filled with tile samples for my daughter."

Alanna added. "He was awake all night because he bought the factory. He slept all the way. I called him a sleepyhead."

Clay laughed heartily and agreed. "Yes. Alanna is right. I slept from Chicago to Downers Grove. I'm still a bit tired. Krystal, this is John."

Krystal asked, "You knew my name?"

John nodded, "Something I learned from Clay. He has a great memory; after meeting Clay I've tried to be better at recalling names."

Clay grinned and said, "So, John, please tell us all the news. We all want to know what we're dealing with."

Krystal thought; this is something! Clay has been awake for maybe twenty minutes, and he has created a very impressive warm relationship with all three girls and he has promised them that he would not abandon them.

The conductor shrugged and began, "Frank's name is Franklin Dickerson. He pretended to be the brother of the girl's father. Posing as their uncle when their parents were killed, he took responsibility of the girls, and after selling the house and everything in it, he bought train tickets as far as Naperville. His plan was to dump the girls and run. Then he saw your heavy bag, figuring it was full of gold, and decided to steal what he thought was your gold and leave the girls behind."

Clay asked, "Why did he think there was gold in the satchel?"

"He overheard the ticket seller call you Hangdog and he also spoke of your gold mine."

Krystal smiled and asked, "Pardon me. What is your nickname?"

Clay laughed and spoke. "For years, evidently because of the seriousness of my facial expression, I've been nicknamed Hangdog. Can you see why?"

Krystal thought that her first impression was a very serious facial expression, but the moment he spoke, smiled, or laughed, his look was warm and accepting. After talking about being serious, she wondered about her own facial expression lately. She smiled at the thought that Clay could laugh at an expression that wasn't complementary, instead he embraced the name.

Clay smiled and directed some clarification toward Krystal. "John, this is Krystal Kenworth, our neighbor and a very kind lady. Someone who I think we will have to beg for her assistance now and then. Krystal, John was a Chicago cop. He chose to quit that job so he could talk with wonderful people like yourself. Today, he ended up having to deal with Frank."

John smiled and explained, "Clay, I told you that story a year ago. You've got a wonderful memory, and you recalled my name. So, what is my wife's name? "

Clay grinned and related, "Janel, you have two kids, the oldest boy loves to play softball."

John laughed and shook his head, "What a great memory."

"Now, John, the envelope you handed me?"

The conductor nodded. "The envelope contains what is left of the proceeds from the sale of the kids' house."

Clay asked, "The tickets that Frank purchased for the kids, how far ahead did he purchase?"

The conductor shook his head, "Just to the next stop. Naperville."

Clay responded, "Ok. We'll need tickets for the girls all the way to Denver. I'll also need another sleeping car for the girls, preferably on the lowest level. Close to mine. If you cannot get one right away, I'll sleep sitting in the booth with the porter so I can be close."

Krystal smiled at Clay's obvious concern for the three girls, he'll perhaps have to give up his sleeping birth for the girls and he is willing to do so.

The conductor asked, "Anything else?"

"How long do we stop at Naperville?"

John responded, "About 35 minutes."

"Do they have a department store there? We need a lot of things for the girls."

John shook his head. "I'm not sure."

Krystal added, "Yes, they do. It is well equipped."

Clay gave Audrey a hug, looked at Krystal and said, "Krystal, can you help us?"

Krystal noted that Audrey was starting to smile, perhaps trust was building, impulsively she reached to Audrey and took her hands and asked, "Of course I'll help. Audrey, we are going to have to move fast, we'll need your help. Are you ready to go shopping with us, Audrey? We will have to do some fast buying. Clothes, night clothes, jackets, socks, shoes…" Krystal again smiled when she received an enthusiastic nod from Audrey.

Carl watched Audrey respond to Krystal and figured that Krystal's motherly approach was well accepted by Audrey. Carl sincerely spoke, "Great. Krystal. I am so very glad you are here."

Andrea gave Krystal a momentous hug; Krystal thought she was getting the better end of the exchange. Needy children were showing their appreciation. Alanna followed suit with a longer-duration hug that turned into a cuddle. Krystal thought about the smiles she enjoyed and produced, loving touches of the girls, the laughing… as she thought about Carl's very warm and giving response to the girls… she wondered about… love?

John asked, "Can you think of anything else?"

Clay shrugged, "Not that I can think of right now. If we think of anything, we'll let you know. And John, I want to sincerely thank you for everything."

The conductor started to get up then said, "Before I go, I'm very happy to tell you three girls this. Clay and Krystal are two of the nicest people in the world. Don't be afraid to go to them with any problem you have. With these two, you are in the best of hands."

Krystal, while still holding Alanna, asked. "Thank you for including me, John, but how…?"

The conductor smiled, "I got the word from the ticket salesman. He had a lot of praise for you and your ability as a businesswoman, a great lady, and a community builder. I think you two will be able to handle this situation very well."

Alanna, while sitting on Krystal's lap, announced. "I'm hungry."

Clay hastily dug out a pencil and paper and said, "John, before you go, I have to have you, and Krystal sign a statement witnessing that I will put $700 in the bank for the girls."

The conductor questioned. "But I only gave you $312."

Clay nodded. “Yes, I know; I just decided to double the amount.”

After the signing was completed, Clay asked, “Krystal, would you like to dine with us?”

Krystal smiled broadly. She was almost in tears at the joy of being able to simply smile a few times, and she had hope there was good, loud laughter ahead. “Yes, Clay. I would love to dine with you and the girls.” Krystal thought about the doctor’s advice, ‘find someone just as nice as she…

Clay took Audrey’s hand and asked, “Krystal, how far are you traveling?”

Krystal answered, “I purchased tickets to Denver.”

Clay asked, “Great. Do you have friends in Denver?”

With Alanna taking one of her hands and Andrea taking her other hand, Krystal answered with a big smile. “Well, I figure there will be you, your wife, and the three girls for a starter.”

Clay smiled, “Well, Krystal, my wife passed away a couple of years ago, but I have three super daughters, three grandchildren, and I also have a big house with six bedrooms.”

Krystal thought that things were definitely looking up; she sneakily found out that Clay was available, and she was smiling and chuckling inside at her sly way of finding if Clay had a wife.